Blue an Should Never be Seen!
(or so Mother says)

COLETTE KEBELL

SKITTISH ENDEAVOURS

COLETTE KEBELL

BLUE AND GREEN SHOULD NEVER BE SEEN (Or so Mother Says)
A SKITTISH ENDEAVOURS BOOK:

Originally published in Great Britain by Skittish Endeavours 2015

Copyright © Colette Kebell 2015
First Edition

The right of Colette Kebell to be identified as the author of this work has been asserted in accordance with sections 77 and 78 of the Copyright Designs and Patents Act 1988.

This book is a work of fiction. Names, characters, places and incidents are either the product of the author's imagination or they are used fictitiously. Any resemblance to actual events or locales or persons, living or dead, is entirely coincidental.

Conditions of Sale
This book is sold subject to the condition that it shall not, by way of trade or otherwise, be lent, re-sold, hired out or otherwise circulated in any form of binding or cover other than that in which it is published and without a similar condition including this condition being imposed on the subsequent purchaser.

Skittish Endeavours Books are supplied and printed via Ingram Spark

Printed and bound via Ingram Spark www.ingramspark.com

Thanks to:-
Design © www.Lizziegardiner.co.uk; illustrations © Shutterstock.com.
Proof-reader and Copy Editor: Patrick Roberts

For more information on Colette Kebell see her website at
www.colettekebell.com
or
follow her on Twitter @ColetteKebell
and/or
https://www.facebook.com/pages/Colette-Kebell/882613368417057

BLUE AND GREEN SHOULD NEVER BE SEEN!

DEDICATION

Here is where I have to thank my husband. For being my rock, for collaborating, being supportive and for allowing me to bounce around ideas, no matter where they lead to. I would not have been able to get where I am without him

CONTENTS

Contents
CHAPTER 1 7

CHAPTER 2 15

CHAPTER 3 21

CHAPTER 4 29

CHAPTER 5 35

CHAPTER 6 43

CHAPTER 7 50

CHAPTER 8 56

CHAPTER 9 62

CHAPTER 10 69

CHAPTER 11 76

CHAPTER 12 82

CHAPTER 13 89

CHAPTER 14 97

CHAPTER 15 104

CHAPTER 16 112

CHAPTER 17 119

CHAPTER 18 126

CHAPTER 19 131

CHAPTER 20 140

CHAPTER 21 147

CHAPTER 22 157

CHAPTER 23 166

CHAPTER 24 176

CHAPTER 25 183

CHAPTER 26 194

CHAPTER 27 204

CHAPTER 28 212

CHAPTER 29 218

CHAPTER 30 225

CHAPTER 31 234

CHAPTER 32 240

CHAPTER 33 246

CHAPTER 34 254

CHAPTER 35 265

CHAPTER 36 274

CHAPTER 37 284

CHAPTER 38 292

CHAPTER 39 299

CHAPTER 40 306

CHAPTER 41 313

CHAPTER 42 319

CHAPTER 43 325

CHAPTER 1

Norwegian jumpers for Christmas? Oh, come off it! I do have some ethics, after all.

This guy is driving me nuts.

You might think the decline started in 2008, when the recession hit us all, but actually no. The BIG problem started when I decided I could improve the world by expanding my business. Adding a male section to my personal shopping website seemed the right thing to do at that time. After all, why limit my expertise to only half of the world? I was wrong – no, I was deeply wrong, on so many levels.

At first people thought, unbelievably and for whatever reason, that it was a dating website and spammed me. "Hey, is it you in that picture?" or, even worse, "What size are you?" Among those, there was the odd genuine person who would have benefited from some style advice. But let's be frank: they were only a few. Despite my polite answers (after all, I am a Personal Shopper) I soon realised there was no hope.

The latest request, received today, was from a Jasper Barnes, allegedly working as an entrepreneur in London, asking me to find him a Norwegian jumper. Size was included in the email. Personally, I don't have anything against Norwegian jumpers. Some of them are beautiful. My best friends wear them. The problem is how to explain to a grown-up man that those sweaters make you look like Pippi Longstocking's Norwegian uncle. May I offer you some reindeer jerky while you're waiting?

Being a personal shopper is a dark art, with few tangible rewards. With the business spread by word of mouth, my clients would never admit they needed my assistance. Not even if they were put under torture. Let's be honest: who would admit to being in need of a style consultant?

People need advice, and, often a fresh point of view helps in rejuvenating a wardrobe that, with time, has become boring. But would they admit it? Not a chance!

It's like being an alcoholic: the first step is to admit you need help, and acknowledge that that pair of leggings, now you're in your mid-fifties, don't suit you any more. When you have recognised that, you're on the road to recovery, and my services will help you.

I started by chance, when I was in my late twenties. I'm a compulsive shopper, and I don't mean that in a derogatory way. The right to shop should be up there in the constitution (if I still lived in America, that is), just below the "free exercise of religion" and the "freedom of speech", and above the "right to keep and bear arms" (unless they come in different colours).

A sort of Amendment 1B: *Congress shall make no law in respect of the free exercise of shopping; or abridging the freedom of a shopping spree; or the right of the people peaceably to assemble (except during the sales period), and spend on clothes and shoes. Banks shall invest in the people's right to their pursuit of happiness, by means of fashion design.*

So the big question is, do I satisfy a potential customer – someone who might have thousands of pounds to spend – and forget my beliefs? Is it worth bending my ethics to please a client, just because we are in a post-recession period (and I actually need the money)?

The simple answer is, "NO. Never. Not a chance in hell. Zilch."

Dear Jasper,

Thank you for contacting me at GiGi-Personal Shopper. I reviewed your request for helping you to find a Norwegian jumper for this Christmas but, unfortunately, I have to decline the request.

As a Personal Shopper, I should inform you that we do not shop for specific items upon request. We prefer a more personal approach, where we spend time understanding our customer needs and have a full review of their current style in order to then propose suitable alternatives. It's a slow process, I suppose, that would not fit your requirements.

I appreciate the difficulties you might have encountered in finding the above-mentioned item. To be honest, I recollect my grandfather having one, a long time ago, but since then they seem to have entirely disappeared from the face of the earth.

I definitely have in my memory a scene from the Norwegian film "Troll i Ord", 1954, where they wear one. Since "The Eiger Sanction" (starring Clint Eastwood, 1975), where the main character moved on to wearing a neck jumper, fashion seems to have evolved, somewhat, inexplicably.

I asked my partner to research the matter, and I understand there are niche markets for the item you requested. Please see the attached list for websites and shops (mostly in Norway) that could fulfil your desire for tradition.

Warmest (if you find your jumper) regards

GiGi Griswald.

You might have wondered about my surname. My dad is Swedish with perhaps a sprinkle of German (hence the surname), while my mother is actually Italian. We also have a pinch of Maltese and French somewhere in our ancestry, but that's another story. I took my passion for clothes and fashion from my mother; otherwise, I would have had my own flat-pack clothes shop by now. What I found funny is that they called me Griselda, which means "Dark Battle" or some such in German. The reason behind that is still a mystery, and the two are not willing to give up the secret anytime soon.

I grew up in New York until I reached my tenth birthday, and then the family went back to Milan for a couple of years. The latter period was fundamental to my fashion imprinting, before we moved to the UK.

In my mid-twenties, I had what "they" call a credit-card problem. To me, it wasn't an issue at all, and although I admit I was late with my payments, I thought I was exercising my rights, as per Amendment 1B above. Unfortunately the Bank Manager, a little sad man with no sense of imagination or social compassion, thought otherwise. He gave me an ultimatum: repay your debts or else!!

At that time, I was working for a small firm of solicitors in Berkshire and I hated every minute of it. At school I wasn't great – not bad, but definitely not great. I found that many of the subjects were boring, or at least they were presented as such. No wonder I failed my GCSE in Domestic Economy – except I then become one of the most influential fashion trendsetters (not the dog) in the kingdom. Yeah, there is that little detail that I'm still not super-rich, but hey, the business is thriving, so no complaints there.

After a family meeting in my teens, we (?) decided that, owing to my non-bright school career, I should settle for a less demanding profession, and eventually the word "secretary" came out of someone's mouth; I don't remember whose. I was indeed fast at typing and quite smart, and during those years of teen-laziness, the job suited me well. Earning money was no longer an issue, except for the fact that I like shopping.

Yeah, you bet: by the tenth of the month I had made many shopkeepers happy. In some cases, I think I even contributed to sending some of their children to university, considering the amount of money I spent. Something needed to be done. In order to be successful in life, you need to have a plan. I had one, although maybe mine wasn't the smartest one.

My plan followed the dictate of the major business universities of the world, such as Harvard and Oxford, and was a "best of breed" in the industry. It was simple, clear and concise: I needed more money. As you can imagine, that didn't take me very far; after all, I was still a simple secretary. But even in the world of secretariat, people can progress and enhance. There are CEOs all over the country who need a bright mind to sort out their mess – what they call a Personal Assistant, which is nothing other than a secretary with a posh name and a hefty salary. You name it, the world was my oyster, and I only needed the right knife and right technique to open that damn mollusc. I needed to find my niche.

The first objective was really quite simple: find a job, get some experience under my Ferragamo pink belt, and then move on to a higher-paid job. After one year of window-shopping and struggle, I was ready to make my move. And so I did. The new job was paying a substantial three thousand pounds more a year (gross) than my first one. No more rummaging in the TK Maxx sale bargain bucket, like a homeless person in search of that discarded treasure in the bin, which never comes. No more scavenging the Primark department store in search of that shirt that, if well matched with a proper skirt and accessory, will not look cheap. Maybe I could even avoid delaying buying until the sale season. To be honest, I quite liked the word "season" associated with the sale one. That was a perfect description of me – a real bargain hunter, who lets the prey's population grow until it's time, and then goes in for the kill.

The reality hit me in the face two pay packets later, when I realised there was this guy going around called "Mr Inflation", who took all the fun out of my hard-earned, well-deserved salary. "Mr Inflation": a kryptonite who sucked all the spending power out of my wage.

The bastard.

A revised strategy was soon due, so I started working some evenings and weekends as a nanny. It wasn't going to earn much, or change my life, but, it gave a bit of oxygen to my finances, although I knew from the start that it would be more like the last breath on a sinking "Titanic" rather than a fresh breeze in the spring. But I landed distinctly well, with a Pakistani family not far from where I lived. At that point, I was still living with my parents in a decent-sized house near Bray. The neighbourhood was wealthy and in need of good, trustworthy nannies who could guard the precious and beloved children while their parents went out for a boozy night. They were family friends, lived across the road, and with a small push from Mum, there you go. I was hired.

CHAPTER 2

Despite working extra hours in a rich neighbourhood, don't get too excited; they don't pay much. With the extra money, now I could afford Clarks, not leaving a scratch on the huge, thick, bullet-resistant glass of high fashion. However, the job proved to be – how should I say? – rewarding. The girls were good fun to look after, Daddy was often around the world for business or taking Mommy out for a business meal and Mommy … well, Mommy was in need of some serious help. But let's not digress yet. The two girls were Laila and Uzma, of eight and ten years of age respectively. Two pretty angels with long, dark hair and deep brown eyes that would be easily satisfied with a few games played in the evening and a bowl of ice cream. We usually played in the lounge, a huge space with more sofas than a furniture shop and paintings that should have been, actually, in a museum. The odd piece of sculpture was scattered around the house, and the girls knew well enough that they should avoid dangerous games like football or tennis inside the house. Not that they didn't do it, but at least they understood they had to be careful. That made my job extremely easy.

However, most of the time, it was enough to entertain them with a game of cards, Pictionary or hide-and-seek. Considering I was working there in the evening, the girls became tired soon enough to allow me to send them to bed. Quite often I still had time, before the parents' return, to catch up with "What Not to Wear" on telly with Trinny and Susannah, my personal superheroes on a mission to save the world from bad clothing.

I remember clearly – it will stay imprinted in my mind for the rest of my life – one evening in the summer when we played hide-and-seek. Laila, the younger girl, decided to hide in Mommy's wardrobe. They knew the rooms upstairs were off limits, except for their own, but after a long time spent hunting for her in the usual places, I had to give up and expand my search. I had to start searching the master bedroom and at that point I realised the full horror of what I saw, in front of these very eyes, when I opened the wardrobe doors.

They say that before dying one can see one's own life passing by, like in a movie, before one's eyes. What was in front of me was the most horrific scene I had ever experienced: a huge walk-in wardrobe full of the most ghastly set of clothes I could ever imagine. I was speechless, paralysed, and I could hardly breathe. They were the sort of attire my grandmother could wear to a wedding party, if she felt she didn't like the bride much. Pastel-coloured outfits with gigantic buttons on the top. I thought vinyl was abandoned years ago in favour of CDs and MP3s, but apparently some people still use those old records somewhere; well, it was the same here, transposed into the world of fashion. Those clothes could have been very good for our beloved Queen in her eighties, but come off it; Mommy was barely in her thirties! One in particular horrified me: a blue and yellow sequined dress with humungous pink flowers all over the place. I poked it with a stick from a distance to ensure it wasn't alive and ready to kill me. You know, sometimes they haunt you. Could these really be her clothes, or were they keepsakes from an old, deceased aunt?

Well, that gave little Laila the opportunity to sneak away and win the game, but at that point I started questioning the parenting skills of the couple. Seriously, letting a little girl hide inside that eyesore? I thought for a brief moment about calling social services; how could I save the two little girls from a style-less future?

No, this was something that needed a deeper approach; I would have to protect these poor little creatures by addressing the issue at the source: the mother. Marianne was a fine woman, an affectionate mother and a generous person; she had been born in Denmark and was a good friend of our family, although for whatever reason, she and her husband didn't often come to our house. I would dare say she was a perfect woman, living a perfect life – that is, except for her taste in clothes matters. If money can't buy happiness, it certainly can't buy style, that's for sure. I assessed that she was in that awkward situation when, after a few years spent caring for the family, she had slowly moved into that phase of life where people enjoy being "comfortable". The worst fashion crimes in history have been committed in the name of "comfort". Comfortable is the Jack the Ripper of style, and soon afterwards comes the loss of interest, the divorce and a life of misery spent feeding the pigeons, alone in the park, or worse, sharing your life with 20 cats.

Don't get me wrong: she had loads of money and she could buy expensive stuff; she was just purchasing the wrong style. I was ready to explore another cunning plan of mine, on how to approach her, when she gave me a lifeline. "Oh, Griselda," she said one day when I had just arrived at her place for another evening of babysitting (I didn't really think about it as "babysitting", rather like a donation to my shoes fund), "you always dress so smartly; you must have spent a fortune." Indeed I was dressed smartly, but I guess we had a different concept of what "spending a fortune" consisted of.

"I wouldn't say that. The top was just twenty pounds. The leather trousers are Nicole Farhi, but I got them from an outlet. They're actually a sample, so you won't see another pair around," I said.

"Really? Are you saying that is a unique piece?" The bait was cast and the big fish was going to swallow it, hook, line and sinker.

"Sure: there are plenty of places, if you know where to look, and with your figure I guess it wouldn't be difficult to find something for you. Of course, only if you're interested …" I could see her thoughts spinning around in her head. On the one side, there was the opportunity of having a less out-of-date wardrobe and, for once, not looking in your thirties as if you had the same fashion designer as our beloved Queen. On the other side, she was a rich woman; she couldn't afford to be seen in one of the bargain shops and outlets I used to hunt in. Appearance is everything, they say. I threw a lifeline for her. "You don't have to buy anything, and if someone sees you, you can always say you were accompanying me …"

She mulled it over for a moment, the doubts eating her flesh from the inside while she was pondering the risks-to-benefits ratio. Then, eventually: "What about this Saturday?"

"Saturday, it is. You'll love it!"

CHAPTER 3

"What do you mean by 'He's back!'?" I asked Ritchie, who was waiting by my office sheepishly.

"Jasper, Norwegian-jumper guy, is back. He wrote another email."

"Ritchie, come on, you know I don't have time for this. Give him a generic answer and tell him, nicely, to go to hell."

"I tried, actually. We've already exchanged a dozen emails. He wants you." He put his index finger on his lips, as he always does when he's thinking if it's a case of telling me the whole truth, or not.

"OK, spit it out! What's going on?" I asked eventually.

"He's cute," he said with that guilty face and puppy-dog eyes, knowing very well he'd touched a forbidden topic.

I have known Ritchie for donkeys' years, way back from high school, and we've been best friends ever since. We share a passion for clothes and everything that's fashionable. That gave him some trouble back then: the way he dressed was a bully magnet. At that age you have to be grey and conform to the uniform like the others; any deviation caused you to be a target. The fact that he was quite camp and openly gay didn't help his case. At that time I was a bit of a tomboy, and I couldn't stand all those intimidators around him; I had to fight. I even went to the extent of bashing one around the head with an umbrella. The fact that I was a girl, and my brother was the toughest kid in the area, avoided further retaliations. Ritchie and I have been friends ever since, and he was my first and only choice when I decided to open this business. Sometimes he brings me back to reality; he's the one who also helps me to manage our poor finances, and keeps me in line when I'm overspending. And no, even if I am the boss, I'm not – if you know what I mean.

"Are you still trying to find me a boyfriend, by any chance?" I teased him, trying to wear my grumpy face.

"You should listen to me. The last ones you had were mostly failures," he countered.

"Yeah, thanks. How come you always say that

after we split up, and never give a warning in time?" That was typical of him.

"You have to learn from your mistakes, darling. What kind of friend would I be if I have to bitch about all your love affairs? No, dear: now you're on your own. You will die alone and grumpy," he laughed back.

"Yeah, sure. What about Norwegian-jumper guy; what does he want?" I questioned him.

"He needs the help of your fashion expertise – what else?"

Something wasn't right. "How do you know he's cute?"

"The message is in your inbox, darling, and there's a full picture. And if you don't want him, I'll take him." Be my guest, I thought: take him. Have a nice marriage in jumperland, and don't come back to me begging for mercy and pleading to take you back. I'll have them put you in retail rehab for at least six weeks.

Dear Griselda

I am the first to admit when I make a mistake and I realised I have done so (you see? I am open-minded after all). I understood what you wanted to tell me from the beginning. Now I know and I completely gave up the search for a Norwegian jumper. I still like them, don't get me wrong, but it's clear they wouldn't suit my personality. That's how great you are. You were able to make me look inside; discover my real nature and, most of all, dare!

I am a new person, thanks to you. I finally understood the underlying message you were trying to convey. I have been inspired by your example and I wanted to share with you a photo of the new me. Thanks to you, I feel we now can speak as peers. Two enlightened individuals sharing the same battles.

Thank you again.

Jasper, your co-equal.

WHAT-THE-FROCK? I could not believe my eyes! The guy was fitted out with a brown squared tweed jacket, go-cycling trousers and woollen socks. Red. The black shoes seemed the only reasonable thing in what otherwise would have appeared as the perfect picture of Tinker's grandson, straight out of Lovejoy. He even had the damn bow tie.

"Ritchieeee! Are you winding me up with this guy?" I shouted from my office. "Be honest, is this a friend of yours?"

Ritchie got up from his chair and walked, very slowly, towards my office. His back was straight, his head slightly inclined back, in his best "disgusted" attitude. If I didn't know he was doing the upset game, I could have sworn he was saddened by my insinuation.

"What makes you think I've had anything to do

with all this?"

"Well, the list is long. First, we have a history of you trying to get me dates. Remember a few months ago, that department store manager you wanted me to meet?"

"Guilty as charged!" continued Ritchie, shamefaced. "But he was cute."

"And gay! We passed the evening talking about YOU!"

"… Erm …"

"Are you guys still seeing each other?" I asked. I was actually curious to know if at least it ended well.

"No: I guess we had some discrepancies; we couldn't work it out, eventually. But … his personality would have fitted with you and …"

I interrupted him; I knew very well that he was trying to dodge a bullet. "And the one before that?" I added inquisitively.

"Yes, but …"

"No but! There are moments when you sound like my mother. You need a family, someone to share your life with, buying a house …" I continued.

"Which you haven't managed to do yet," he said. "You might be the first woman who doesn't have any bedrooms in her apartment – just walk-in wardrobes."

Now he was pissing me off: he always does when he's right. I didn't pay much attention to my love life; it always came last in my list of priorities –

after my job, after my friends. For God's sake, even after my wardrobe. The outcome was simple: my love life was a disaster. Paying too much attention to "the partner matter" always ended up in tears. Well, I assume that, for whatever reason, my fixation with clothes and shopping might have contributed, although I'm not entirely sure why. Having placed my love life on such a low level in my list of priorities, I ended up with wrong choices, partners too different from me, a boring one or a psychopath in search of attention. I also had a crush on Ritchie years ago, despite knowing he was gay. Now we're good friends, but I think he knows and maybe that's why he's making an effort to help me find the man that (in his words) I deserve. I shrugged and went back to the question I had on my hands. This Jasper fellow.

Dear Jasper, my co-equal

I welcome you into the fantastic world of fashion and personal shopping assistance. I now see the potential in you, although I would have accessorised your outfit also with a Benelli shotgun and a golden retriever. But that's just me.

I hope for you all the best and good luck.

Warmest regards,
GiGi Griswald

Ritchie was reading over my shoulder and was fuming and shaking his head, disapprovingly.

"You really didn't think that …" I started saying.

PLING!

Dear Griselda

What about meeting for lunch tomorrow? Let's say at 12.30 pm at Café Rouge; it's very close to your office, so it wouldn't be too much of a hassle.

Just a coffee and a chat. I'm not asking for anything else.

Jasper

"He's persistent, this little fellow." I said, looking up at Richie, who was biting his nails to the bone. "He doesn't even know if I'm married or what and …" Then I clicked.

"RITCHIE! WHAT DID YOU TELL HIM ABOUT ME? NO, YOU COME BACK HERE RIGHT NOW … DON'T YOU DARE …"

He was gone. I will catch you later, I thought. You can run, but you can't hide. Not with that loud Cavalli shirt, you can't.

Dear Jasper

Fine.

Warmest regards,
GiGi Griswald

CHAPTER 4

And so I went shopping with Mommy Marianne. We had to skip altogether a couple of charity shops in Sunningdale, where I had previously found some decent bargains. Rich people in the area donate their little-used items to charity and often you can find a good selection of designer clothes. I'm not worried if they're second-hand; quite often they're unused altogether – bought on impulse and sitting in a wardrobe for ages, and then donated to make space for new ones. Some of them have the year of manufacture written all over them and are to be avoided. On the other hand, occasionally you can find a timeless piece, that unique shirt or garb (rarely skirts, though, for some unknown reason) that still appear fresh and novel today. They would look fashionable even in ten years' time, in my opinion.

But obviously the idea of being caught looking at clothes in a charity shop was too much for Marianne: a mistake I should have envisaged and prevented. No, the lady would only consider new items.

And so we drove further, to Windsor. Marianne was a bit reluctant at the beginning; she knew those shops inside out and she could never find anything that could even interest her. And mostly they were chain shops; same stuff all over the country.

I didn't mind the objections; I knew what I was doing. We left the car in the big parking lot by the train station and walked towards Peascod Street. Marianne was unimpressed.

Finally we turned left, just before the station, and there it was – a small shop with just two windows. On the outside there were Iron Maiden T-shirts, and others depicting red double-decker buses, or the British flag. In the main window, there were also mugs and other tourist items.

"Did you just bring me to a tourist gift shop?" asked Marianne in disbelief, uncertain if she wanted to cross the threshold and enter.

"Shhh, this is a gift shop, but of another kind. Follow me." I winked at her. Eventually she entered and started looking around.

"GiGi, how're you doing?" I was greeted by one of the assistants as soon as he spotted me and he kissed me on the cheeks.

"I'm doing very well, Tony. How's the family?" I asked

"Much of the same, apart from the little one, who keeps me awake. She has decided to join the Twilight Saga crew, staying awake at night and sleeping during the day. Definitely gets that from her mother, who keeps sucking the blood out of my finances."

"We need access to The Vault!" I whispered to him, pointing my head in Marianne's direction.

"Are you sure? I remember last time you went to the dungeon you didn't emerge from it unscathed. Well, your finances didn't, that is."

"I know, but this time I've brought reinforcements. Mind you, she might be your best client ever, with a bit of help," I said, looking in the general direction of Marianne, who was now paying attention to an Iron Maiden T-shirt depicting a demon riding a horse.

"Sure: you two follow me." I made a sign to Marianne that the time had come, and she followed us to the back of the shop, with a perplexed look stamped on her face. He opened a metal door and led the way through a series of steps going down to the warehouse, a vast area probably built at the same time as the train station.

We were entering the sancta sanctorum of undercover style, the dark net of the fashion industry, where samples and originals could be bought or exchanged in utmost secrecy.

Not spitting out your sources was the secret of success, and probably Marianne was not fully aware of how much I was sharing with her. Down in The Vault, racks upon racks of clothes and accessories were lined up, occasionally thrown in large containers that someone would have to dive into to search for that elusive item.

Marianne was flabbergasted; her eyes were lost in the multitude of colours, shirts and accessories surrounding us. A few women were scattered around the shop and they turned their heads to observe the newcomers, giving us angry looks, as if we were threatening their search – intent on discovering that precious item before they could. Down there, sizes were a luxury and often clothes came in a single size. Waiting too long was also not an option and one should make her mind up quickly. Things were snatched in a matter of seconds; that's why, if you found something suitable, you clung onto it until you were a hundred per cent sure you wanted to buy it or else let it go. It was not unheard of for a person contemplating a skirt to leave it aside for a few minutes while looking for something else, only to find it had been grabbed by someone else. The place could be tense, at times.

Marianne was lost: no granny clothes in here, so she had to use her imagination. She picked up a dress that had an almost full circular skirt to it, and she even tried it on. How to break the news gently? All those folds in the fabric … not good when you want to hide a rather large backside. It was indeed a good one, but not suitable for her. The advantage was that she was tall and mostly slim, but … erm … her bottom was a bit oversized and that dress was making it look even bigger.

Something needed to be done, but how to make her understand she was making a mistake? I opted for the diplomatic solution, bringing her a pair of dark Fendi trousers, a shirt and a longer, larger one to wear over the top of it.

"Trust my judgment; this is my domain, after all," I said. She tried the outfit on and she liked it. At that point, I had to explain.

"You see, by wearing this long shirt on top, you make your lines less visible and at the same time they make you look even taller: see for yourself."

"You're right! I can hardly notice my bottom," she said, looking at herself in the mirror, and then turning to one side. "I love it. You know, I've always been aware I was a bit large in the hips, but I never figured out what I could have done. It's brilliant."

She made a move to try a large belt on top of that beautiful cream shirt and I had to stop her. "You see, if you add a belt, then you go back to square one, and make your lines visible again. That's something you should avoid like …"

"Oh, my God! I've just realised my wardrobe is all wrong …"

She was now becoming self-conscious and understood the horrors that were waiting for her in her wardrobe, at home. I knew the feeling very well, but in my case the excuse was lack of money.

"Don't worry Marianne; it can be sorted out."

We (she) spent over two thousand pounds in the Vault that day and planned another trip for the following Saturday.

A star was born.

CHAPTER 5

Café Rouge it was. I was sitting at an inside table and there was no sign of this Jasper fellow. The waitress was circling around me like a vulture, and she's probably upset because ten minutes have passed and I've not ordered anything yet.

Bummer: he was ten minutes late and I couldn't stand it. It was my time he was playing with. Have you ever thought about how many things you can do in ten minutes, better than sitting in a stupid café waiting for someone who doesn't care?

I did. You could:

– try at least 14 different belts and take a decision;

– queue for a dressing room in Fenwicks and try on at least one shirt;

– analyse one complete rack of clothes in T-K Maxx;

– buy a shotgun, load it, then kill the bastard that kept you waiting and …

Hang on! A nice-looking chap just entered the café and he was looking around; he would be a nice distraction. He was wearing a pair of black shoes that I guess were G J Cleverley. Men's clothes were not my strength, but I was learning fast and the style was unmistakable. For some strange reason the chap was wearing Brandel Blue laces, but they seemed to work just fine. The dark-grey suit fitted him impeccably, tailored for sure, and I was surprised he didn't go for a pin-striped version, but the overall look worked just fine. Probably a Super Wool 150 from the look of it. And the gentleman also seemed to have a nice, juicy bum. If only I was not stuck here waiting …

JASPER? The gentleman turned in my direction and I was shocked. I was expecting him to be wearing a traditional Swiss costume with bells, a nice red-checked farmer's shirt and an alpine hat with flowers all over it – but this? Had he hired another consultant? Was he just trying to wind me up?

Then: "Hi, I'm Jasper." He spoke with a posh accent while he shook my hand firmly. Now that he was right in front of me, I noticed his old Etonian tie – perhaps the only mishap in an almost perfect attire. I would maybe have chosen a JP Gaultier tie in red, but let's not digress – the overall look was impeccable.

He sat and asked if I wanted to eat something. Of course I do, you moron; I'm starving and if it wasn't for you keeping me waiting almost fifteen minutes I would've already murdered a burger.

"Are you going to apologise for being late?" I asked him abruptly.

"Hmm … well … yes, of course; I'm deeply sorry," (he wasn't) "but my previous meeting ran over." Oh dear, now he was going to tell me how important his busy life was and bla bla, bloody bla!

I kept wondering what Ritchie, that little backstabbing Brutus, had told him about me. Did he send him a picture of me? Which one? For sure, the traitor didn't just rely on showing him the one on our website. We stopped that project weeks ago, as we didn't have the funds to go online yet. Maybe one he kept on his mobile? Oh my God, I knew it: he sent him the one where I was dancing on the tables in that Irish pub, drunk as a skunk. What's worse, I was in JEANS!!! That might explain why I had attracted Jasper's attention, for sure a bad style fetishist, dressed by his mum.

Ritchie, my dear friend of olden times, YOU ARE DEAD! And if you aren't yet, I'll kill you with my bare hands once I'm back at the office.

"What are you and Ritchie up to?" I asked, without giving him the chance to poison my ears with his blatant excuses.

"Oh, straight to business? Very well; let's order a bite first, and then I can lay down my commercial proposition." He made a gesture to the waitress, who arrived promptly. He ordered a minute steak with coffee, while I decided in favour of the burger Normandie, which I was going to wash down with a French beer. Did he just say "business proposition"? So this was not a date? What were this guy and Ritchie up to, behind my back? If this guy was an entrepreneur and wanted to buy my business he was definitely out of his mind. Yes, we had a little, tiny, weensy, minuscule issue with cash flow, but that was because we had just opened the office in London. Yeah, OK, we overstretched ourselves and although our customer base was healthy, maybe taking on an office in the capital was more than we could chew at this very moment in time. Hey, but don't they always say in those *Dragon's Den* programmes that you need money to make money, or was that something my mother kept saying? Maybe it was just the profit/turnover ratio? Never mind; the chap in front of me meant business in the literal sense of the term. OK, I offer twenty per cent of the business in exchange for two hundred thousand pounds equity (making my firm worth a hefty million. Here, take that counteroffer, Mr Bannatyne, all coming from Ritchie's share).

"My business proposition is very simple. I'm going to open the largest fashion department store in London; we're renovating a disused warehouse right in front of your office and we're going to shame Bond Street and Mayfair. The Battersea Fashion Centre will be the future destination of millions of shoppers from around the world, getting the best quality at affordable prices – and I've chosen you to run the store. What d'you think?"

What did I think, WHAT DID I THINK, WHAT DID I THINK? He was kidding me! I run my own company, work for myself! I don't know this man from Adam and he wants me to run his little store?

"Jasper, I'm not a store manager. We're a consultancy firm specialising in providing people with new styles, helping them to maximise their looks and appearance. It's a niche market with very specific customers …"

"I know that," he interrupted me, "and that's the beauty of it. You could use your skills to make it a success."

I didn't like it, not one single, little bit – and something sounded odd about his proposition.

"What about my firm? I've invested a lot of time and effort into it …"

"Griselda, we've analysed your business model and it's not scalable. You're, what – barely getting by? Yours is a lifestyle business; I'm proposing you manage the new Harrods of fashion, here in London. I'm not interested in your current business."

WHAT? How dare you! It was true we'd had some financial problems, but hey, we were a start-up company. That was no reason to diminish my business, making it look like a hobby just because he had millions of pounds to spend. Then, he dropped the bomb.

"You'll have an initial salary of a hundred and twenty thousand pounds, plus commission to be agreed upon. Think about it."

My head was spinning. That would allow me to buy a house, a walk-in wardrobe, have a gold credit card to swoosh at every corner. Enough of scraping the barrel and going underground; that would open the door to shops I had dared not enter.

"I'll have to consult my business partner, Ritchie, and see what he thinks."

"Hmm … well … about that: I'm not interested in Ritchie, I'm afraid. He's a nice guy, don't get me wrong, but he's not the kind of person we're looking to hire for our store. Maybe I could give him a basic job as a clerk, on one of the floors?"

No, no, no! This couldn't be happening. Ritchie, out of the game? No way. It was hard for me to admit it – I always pretend that I'm the brains, legs and heart of this venture –but the reality was that I couldn't have done it without Ritchie. He was my partner; we bounced ideas back and forth all the time, and he'd always been there when I needed him. He picked me up when I was on the verge of abandoning everything to stick to a regular job, and he believed in what we were doing as much as I did. And he was my BEST FRIEND.

No way. They could have paid me millions and

I'd have still refused.

"Look, Ritchie is part of …"

"This is not negotiable," he interrupted me, again. Clearly he wasn't interested in what I had to say, and that ended the conversation.

"Very well, Jasper. I'm afraid I have to reject your offer, then."

"I see. You'll regret this, Griselda; you'll be crushed in the process and it's a battle you can't win. Nothing personal: this is business."

How could he sit there and say this wasn't personal? He just didn't get it, did he? This was the very essence of my personality and my life, which was going to be pulverised by a multi-million, multi-national, multi-arsehole business. He was asking me to betray my best friend. This was as personal as it could get!

I opened my purse, put a twenty-pound note on the table to pay for a lunch I hadn't consumed, and left the table. He stood up to shake my hand, but I refused. Exiting, I noticed that his bum was not as great and juicy as I'd first thought.

"How did it go?" asked Ritchie, when I exited the elevator and stormed into my office, barely holding back my tears. "Oh, don't tell me," he continued, "I can see for myself."

He followed me into my office, but he remained standing on the threshold of the door.

"Do you want to talk?" he asked me cautiously.

I explained to him the business proposition,

except for the part about him being left with a simple clerk's job, if he was lucky.

"You must be crazy! I mean, a hundred and twenty grand? Think about how that could change our life, the spin we could give to that place."

"Ritchie, we have something here that we've built together. It might be small, but it's our dream, what we've discussed many times sitting in bars sipping beers. We made that dream come true, our dream come true. I don't want to lose it."

He was upset and started biting his nails, as he always does when he's nervous or mulling something over. You should be edgy, Ritchie, especially if you knew the whole truth.

"Oh, sod it!" he eventually exclaimed. "We'd lose our independence, we'd have to deal with a bunch of tourists who wouldn't appreciate our efforts, and we'd be left with just a hefty amount of money to spend. You know – buying a house, clothes, maybe a car and a place in France for vacationing. How ordinary. It wouldn't be worth it, darling; you made the right decision." And so he went back to his desk.

I knew he was disappointed, but at least he didn't give me a hard time (much). That's what real friends are for. He didn't need to know.

CHAPTER 6

Marianne was the very one who put the seed in my mind. After that initial visit to the underground retail shop, we went to another secret location in Ascot, which specialised in accessories.

She was lost at the beginning, as the place was full of handbags and shoes, and she didn't know where to start. I have to explain one thing to you: I have a photographic memory and also a wardrobe memory, if such a thing exists. Let's clarify this point. If I see something related to fashion, I can remember (and I mean it) the exact colour, size, shop (or the wardrobe) where I saw it and in which rack. I'm not sure how I got this gift, but there it is, possibly something related to the evolution of the species – you know, one of those freaky mutations that happen once in a while in nature and allow the survival of the fittest.

"Look, Marianne, this purple bag would go perfectly with the dress you bought last week." I showed the item with such enthusiasm it almost slipped from my hands. You can't understand what I feel when I find a perfect match. It's pure joy, true romance – like Romeo meeting Juliet, Fred and Ginger, gin and tonic or even the Queen and Prince Phillip. Two items a world apart, from different backgrounds or nations, come together to perfectly fit a woman. Gee, it's like when a bridge is finally finished and the architect contemplates the beauty and the result of his efforts; Leonardo painting the final brush stroke on the Gioconda. It gives a sense of accomplishment that can be felt in your bones, makes you vibrate and resound, finally in harmony with yourself.

Marianne looked at me, embarrassed, and asked, "Which one? We bought so many."

I couldn't believe it; she was almost hopeless. "Come on Marianne: the long dress, the pale-grey, lightweight knitted Ted Baker we found in Windsor, the one with the metallic border that twisted down the front. Can't you see it? – the bag, the clothes and that pair of shoes, the purple and grey square-fronted, peep-toed Nicole Farhi ones with the circular heel that you showed me last week, the ones in your wardrobe on the left side.

At that moment it clicked. I was right in that

obscure place in Ascot and I coined what would become my motto: "The Clothes, the Shoes and the Handbag maketh the woman."

"Yes … ermm … I think you're right. Now I see it." I wasn't completely sure if she actually got it or if she was only going along with me without having a clue what I was talking about. But I didn't really care; I was on a mission to make her look good, stand out from the crowd, become an example for all those women out there who don't have a style. There is hope. You can see the light at the end of the tunnel, and with a little help from your friend GiGi you can also come out on the opposite side safe, sound and beautifully elegant. May the fashion force be with you.

She was still struggling to match items and colours, but she would learn. And if she didn't, I was only a phone call away. We ended our safari a couple of hours later, tired but satisfied with the prey we'd caught.

Her request for help came the following day, when Marianne and her hubby had been invited to dinner by some friends of theirs. I arrived at the house in a hurry, as soon as I'd finished work, but a good hour and a half in advance of when my nanny duty was due to start, and it was pandemonium.

The girls let me in and I ran upstairs, two steps at a time, like a firefighter when someone's life needed saving. The room looked like the aftermath of an explosion: clothes all over the bed, shoes dispersed on the floor – and I could actually see one hanging from the en-suite handle – various items strewn around, unpaired, and Marianne sitting on the floor contemplating the mess. Her eyes were lost in the empty space in front of her and she was repeating, almost chanting, "I can't do it! I can't do it!"

I braced myself and sat down next to her, hugging her. I hoped she wasn't going to start crying, as I couldn't have stood that, and she would definitely have made me cry too (it's infectious!). I needed to keep my calm if I wanted to save the day.

"What seems to be the problem?" I asked tentatively, and she looked at me as if I was an alien.

"I don't remember what goes with what. I tried a few combinations, as you said, but … I don't remember and everything seems so difficult when you aren't around." I caught her before she started sobbing and ruined her make-up.

"Not a problem." I said, very unsure of where to start. I looked at the clutter around me, trying to recognise some familiar items. "You said it's a dinner with friends. How many? I mean, is it a dinner where you sit at a table, or a sort of cocktail party with nibbles etc.?"

She was coming back. "It's sort of a cocktail party, around twenty people – you know the kind of thing, where waiters are going around and you pick what you like from the platters."

"OK! Got it."

Another look around and I knew what I had to do. I picked up a Nougat dress in pale grey with a pastel floral pattern running down one side. What set it off was the silk under-dress, which was barely visible at the bottom, but leaves you feeling rather sexy with the silk next to your skin, and, I paired it up with a pair of Jimmy Choo lamé sandals; the metallic light-grey colour would go perfectly with the bag that I was holding.

"Try this combination and let me know what you think."

She stood up and reluctantly tried the beautiful outfit I showed her, then the shoes and the bag. A big grin spread across her face; eventually she nodded, satisfied. Just the look on her face was worth running there. "My hubby will be happy. He's in the study and he usually refuses to come out until I'm ready. For once I'll be downstairs early; he'll be shocked." She looked around and realised what a state their bedroom was in.

"Don't worry; you go and enjoy your dinner. I can sort this out. Let me know when you're going so I can come downstairs and look after the girls."

"Are you sure? You don't have to do this …"

"Don't worry; it's a pleasure – really." She left the room and I started sorting out the clothes. She had actually made some room in her wardrobe and thrown away the monster clothes. They would probably be sitting in the local charity shop soon, ready to make some old lady happy.

I arranged them by colour – and then it hit me. I ran to the girls' room and asked, "Do you have any labels that you could spare? And a pen?"

The girls were happy to comply and off I went, back to the main bedroom, ready to rock and roll.

After a while Marianne called, to say they were going. I went downstairs to close the door, and guys, I couldn't believe what I saw. Mr Barzani was all affectionate, a sort of hungry Pakistani octopus who had just found its next prey. Marianne grinned and winked at me and off they went.

"Girls, we have a project to do," I shouted from the hallway, once the door was safely closed behind me. "Bring the computer."

It wasn't a working evening, but for a good hour I amused them while trying to work out an Excel sheet, glad that the two girls knew more about computers than I did. We looked at the end results and we were all satisfied. Uzma was in charge of typing and Laila gave her input to make the spreadsheet look pretty, with fancy colours and borders.

Job done.

One Excel spreadsheet listing all the new clothes in a table, while in another two there were the all the bags, shoes, coats and accessories that could be matched. What ingenious work: now you could list what to wear and BANG, you got the answer. Laila suggested we could actually add pictures of all the items, because just with the numbers it wasn't pretty. The girl had a brain, despite her early age.

So then we started a photographic safari. It was a new game and the kids were more than happy to oblige, making my life easier. The expedition ran without any hassle and by ten in the evening we were done. A masterpiece was created.

I sent them to bed and went downstairs to finalise the work. I thought that in addition to the "What to wear" sheet I should have done a "What not to wear" one – the combinations that would definitely lead to a disaster. Those would have given Marianne the opportunity to change and experiment without being bound to my model. I printed the lot and placed it in a folder in her walk-in wardrobe, to be found by Marianne once she returned.

The day after, I learned that the new outfit had earned her a huge amount of praise. Even Mr Barzani demonstrated his appreciation very passionately during the night.

From that moment on, I became her consultant; she also suggested I could buy items on her credit card, or alternatively she would happily pay cash for my effort. She gave me the freedom to go and buy clothes on her behalf. The clothes matrix I prepared proved very useful, freeing her from the dependence of having me around. From nanny, my job had now officially become Fashion Consultant.

CHAPTER 7

"WE GOT A JO-O-O-O-OB!" shouted Ritchie from the other room. Finally! The move to London had almost bankrupted us; we still had a decent number of customers I was serving, but it was definitely not enough. If we wanted to go global, we needed some capital injections from the rich, tasteless women from the capital.

"What kind of job?" I shouted back.

"A rich one, darling. A Lady Whilsham is in need of our services and comes highly recommended by Mrs Lewis, who comes recommended by Mrs Peasmarsh and blahdi blahdi bla …"

"Hey, don't criticise my system! – and bring

Mrs. Lewis' folder. I need to refresh my memory."

The system was simple, but an effective one. I archived a description of each item I bought for each customer, plus a personality profile and a few additional notes on likes and dislikes. While I was bound to secrecy (I don't want to spill the beans, and let new customers know actually how much one of my previous customers needed me), a certain amount of hints were allowed. Not openly saying, but letting it be understood that we, as a firm, had some input in certain matters that we weren't at liberty to discuss, but that made some difference in the end, etc., etc., etc.

"Open a new file on Lady Whilsham. Sounds posh, by the way. What kind of services?" My head was spinning; each new customer was an individual one, posing different challenges – new attire to buy, then soon discover their personalities, what made them what they were. Nothing else in the world smells like that. I love the smell of new customers in the morning.

"Oh, I forgot: Silver, Gold or Platinum?" I asked. We had started classifying our customers the previous year. It wasn't actually based on their wealth, as you might think, but rather on the level of effort required to salvage the situation. Silver meant an easy, short-term consultancy: you know, to bring a lost sheep back onto the right path, while Platinum was reserved for the most desperate cases. They were the ones with orange tans wearing dolls' costumes and blonde hair extensions, the Madonna wannabes, the people who couldn't distinguish grandmother attire from a jute sack.

"This is definitely a Platinum one," squealed Ritchie. "May I come with you this time, darling? Please, please, please: I'm dying of curiosity."

"How do you know that?" I asked, while reading the email Ritchie had just forwarded to me, and not finding any source of information.

"Hellllloooooo? She's from the Royal Borough of Kensington and Chelsea. I know that means nothing to a mountain girl like you, brought down to civilisation by the flood, but here, among advanced and educated people, that means money. Money means spending power in the most luxurious shops in London. If that isn't enough to make a point, she actually needs our help. Well, darling, that is indeed a Platinum."

His reasoning was impeccable and I had no way to retort.

"Very well, Ritchie. We'll work together on this one."

"Oh my love, you won't regret it. Thank you, thank you and thank you!"

We set an appointment for the following Tuesday; we still had a couple of Platinums and a Gold in need of our services that week.

In the meantime the work on the building in front of us started with a fanfare. They erected scaffolding all over it and on top of it, the biggest advertisement one could ever imagine, explaining that the new Battersea Fashion Centre was due to open shortly. The ads depicted shoes and purses, in an attempt to attract the bystanders, promising a world of style for cheap money. Jasper was putting serious money into it and I was worried.

But then it hit me! It wouldn't make any difference to us; we had a very different market. Jasper had missed the very essence of my job. It was true that I could help people to look smart at a reasonable price, but that wasn't the point. All that was already available; there were outlets all over the country, and shops where you could buy inexpensive items were out there too. It was mixing them up in the right way that was the secret. He was just building a huge grocery store, forgetting that the chef is the one who makes the difference. You have to have your own recipes and know how to balance colours. It was like Tesco vs. Heston Blumenthal, the colour factory vs. Vermeer, a brick company vs. Michelangelo. Very different ballparks.

He would make money – more than I could ever imagine – but that wasn't the point. Well, it was in some respects: after all, I was trying to run a business, but what I wanted to say is that I had a vision, a dream, where people could look good without having to spend a fortune; where they could learn and get better at picking clothes and matching them. The Battersea Fashion Centre would only make items available, without teaching anything. That wasn't enough: far from it. I had in my mind the examples of a few customers who had decided to go rogue and not take my advice, and they ended up in tragedy, just to come back begging for help later on. If nothing else, I would have a source of raw material just on my doorstep.

It was time to celebrate our victory, instead of crying with despair. A nice cup of tea was long overdue. I went into the kitchen and brewed one for myself and one for Ritchie.

"This evening we have to celebrate our victory against Goliath, my dear friend," I said, putting the cup of tea on his desk "Let's have a party!"

He turned his head away from the computer and, with a sceptical look on his face, asked "What? Did you win the lottery that you aren't even playing?"

I didn't believe in the lottery; he was right. I was a firm believer that people make their own destiny and for the majority of us that means working hard and making our dreams come true.

"No, I didn't. It's even better than that."

"An American uncle died and left you millions? You got a contract from the government asking you to design the new army uniforms? Because that I would like. Imagine having to do field trips where I have to cope with all those naked soldiers in front of me. That would be a sartorial dream."

"No, it's even better than that too." While I explained my plot, Ritchie's jaw started dropping. I didn't know at that point if he fully realised what I was saying – my vision, The "Master Plan".

"Darling, I'm not sure what you put in that tea of yours, but I want some as well."

He was sceptical, of course. I was sceptical, too.

"Come on – the firm will pay for the party."

"In that case, you're a genius." We both laughed loudly and decided that we were done for the day. It was time for celebration.

CHAPTER 8

"Today we celebrate victory against the empire of evil and bad taste. It has been a long battle and a few of our credit cards and savings accounts perished in the process. Their sacrifice will not be in vain and they will be remembered – mostly because the bank keeps sending those annoying payment notes through the post. We feared for a moment for our lives, but Ritchie and I came out of it safe and sound. We're here to stay, and to work for a better-dressed world. May the force (of fashion) be with you."

I admit, I'd had a couple of tequilas too many, but I meant every single word of it – whatever I said: I'm not so sure I remember. We had invited a dozen of our friends and that, perhaps, was a mistake, considering Ritchie's worried face at the mounting drinks tab. But hey, for once I felt confident that our enterprise was on the right track; we had to celebrate.

I met Ritchie's boyfriend that evening as well, after months of shilly-shallying: a Jonathan Rupert. Rupert was his surname. Probably Ritchie had felt he was the right one and avoided presenting him to me for fear of my passing bad judgement. He's never been like that – ah, the love. Jonathan was a nice chap with a Mediterranean look and dressed in a grey suit; he was probably an "Armanian". He had a part-time job in a coffee shop, while for the rest of the day he worked as an unsuccessful fashion designer. I felt he was already part of the family: he was indeed of our breed, spending his hard-earned salary on his appearance.

They were a nice couple, and as soon as Ritchie started circling around me, trying to guess my approval or denial, I put him at ease by gesturing a thumbs-up. It was none of my business, to be honest, but I just wanted to see him happy and I thought he surely was.

Further down were Helena and Adam, talking with Anne-Marie. The couple I've known since I was a kid, and Helena actually grew up in the same road as Ritchie and me: my two oldest mischievous friends. She wasn't from a rich family, but when you're a kid those things have little significance in life. We were as thick as thieves and inseparable.

For some unknown reason she had a south London accent that made her mumble most of the time, making it hard to understand what she was actually saying. Adam, on the other hand, came from a family with old money and he was as posh as could be, although if one could forget his heritage, he was actually a down-to-earth guy. After an undisclosed number of elocution lessons, Helena was finally ready to be presented to the family and became Adam's wife. Despite as much effort as they could muster, from the parents of both sides, to divide them, they were in love and thriving. In five months' time she would give birth to their first child and that was an even better reason for celebrating tonight.

Anne-Marie was also an old friend. We had met at school when her parents moved to England from France. Wine started becoming more popular in the UK and her father spotted a business opportunity in the import/export sector, making him one of the most influential distributors of French wine in the country. Anne-Marie and I clicked from the very beginning and soon afterwards I introduced her to my circle of friends.

A few other old friends were around that evening too, mostly from school, with the exception of Marianne, the most amazing talent scout I could ever hope to meet.

Ritchie and I had a few gifts to share with our dear friends (who, incidentally, were also our involuntary marketing managers occasionally) that evening and after another round of drinks, we made a sign to the waiter, who helped us to hide the treasure.

During the previous few weeks, we had reached an agreement with a few underground distributors to have a first sneak peek whenever they received new designs or samples. They didn't need convincing, considering how much our customers or we spent in their shops and, therefore, it was actually a no-brainer. On the other side, being the first to have access to their new arrivals was a strategic advantage for us: less struggle for sizes, less of a kerfuffle to continue visiting shops that, frankly, were not exactly on our doorstep. In addition, as we had spent a few pennies to develop a proper computer program to manage our customers and their inventories, we had the possibility of instantly matching any new arrival to what our customers already had and therefore being proactive.

The program was developed professionally, not a botched job made by two IT incompetents like Ritchie and I. A top-notch R&D developer from Hewlett Packard called Spencer made it; he happened to be married to an old friend of mine, Jasmine, who also happened to share my passion for fashion. Women can be extremely convincing, at times. As far as I understood, the negotiation went like this:

- [Jasmine]: This friend of mine will need your help with a custom-built program, one you surely can do easily, to manage a clothes inventory.

- [Spencer]: (while watching telly) Hmmmm.

- [Jasmine]: I also found Hillary is going to the designer outlet in Ashford next week, I might tag along.

- [Spencer]: OK, I got the point, but not now: I'm watching football.

- [Jasmine]: Surely those carpets look disgusting, don't you think? We should think of changing them one of these days.

- [Spencer]: Yes, but why don't …

- [Jasmine]: … And the kitchen would benefit from a coat of paint. You promised that months ago.

- [Spencer]: Hmmm.

- [Jasmine]: You're a computer genius; surely it can't be too difficult to write a simple program for my dear friend.

- [Spencer]: Do we have to talk now? Spurs are playing …

- [Jasmine]: … And the shed's a mess. We should do a trip to the dump this weekend, sorting out all that wood and rubbish you have in there.

- [Spencer]: Ermm …

- [Jasmine]: I was looking at our finances, and maybe we could cut that Sky Sports subscription, you know. Since we've had it, nothing is getting done in this house, maintenance-wise.

- [Spencer]: I'll do it one of these evenings, whe …

- [Jasmine]: You know that my car is almost six years old, and it's started making funny noises? I actually think it might be unsafe to drive. We talked about that new Volvo …

- [Spencer]: I'm doing it – now calm down, OK? … See, the laptop is on! And I don't want to be disturbed. Gimme a few days, will ya? (Television off.)

And, as if by magic, the program was delivered in record time. The only thing to do was to fill it with all the information we had collected and we were ready to "rock and roll". Yeah, of course Jasmine got a big present; who do you think I am?

CHAPTER 9

Following my first assignment, news spread fast, and Marianne's transformation did not go unnoticed. While she had always been the centre of attention, now it was for the right reasons. She had amazed her circle of friends by her transformation, and now the news was that the new Marianne was cool: someone to envy, to look at and wonder about.

But eventually she had to spill the beans to some of her closest friends. Right, she got some help. At the beginning this caused outrage among them, the words "cheating", "deceitful" and "unfair" were thrown in the air a couple of times; but the smartest ones mulled it over, and eventually came to terms with the matter. After all, now Marianne was the star of the show, the one person people were looking at whenever there was a dinner party. Some phone numbers were covertly exchanged, promises not to disclose the secret were made, and from that moment on, I was in business.

The phone call from Marjorie came a few days later. Introduced as Marianne's auntie, she was a woman in her mid-fifties, lived in the Millionaire Street in Crowthorne and shared her mansion with a dozen cats. She was also referred to as "Lady Gaga", for reasons far removed from her musical tastes, and she was a widower. Marianne told me that, after her husband's departure, "Lady Gaga" – how should I say? – let herself down following the dark side of the force. Because my time was precious and I was a young, talented girl in search of her own space in the world, Marianne thought it suitable to inform Marjorie that my services would come at a price – either a flat fee of twenty thousand pounds, all inclusive, or a daily fee of five hundred pounds for a minimum of three weeks, five days a week. In the latter case, Marjorie would have had to pay for the clothes herself. They haggled for a while and eventually settled for eighteen thousand pounds on a flat-fee basis.

I was astounded: even if I spent half of the money on clothes (which sounded unrealistic, considering my bargain underground contacts), that was more than a third of my annual salary.

The doubts started visiting me at night. Blimey,

I would have to file a tax return; and what about my job as a secretary? Would I be able to fulfil the expectations or will it turn into a disaster? The implications were huge: not only could I upset a potential customer, but Marjorie was a relative of Marianne's and it wasn't unheard of for relationships to turn bitter for much less than that.

After a night spent tossing and turning in bed, I found myself resolute in my decision to make this work; on a temporary basis. What do they say in *Dragon's Den* all the time? "Are you prepared to quit your job and dedicate all your energy to this enterprise?" I was indeed, but because I still had almost 20 days of vacation left, I took the safe option of using them instead. I didn't say that, though, to the imaginary Peter Jones asking the damn question.

I explained to my boss that my granny was on the verge of dying after a vast degree of suffering, and there were unavoidable matters I should attend to in Scotland – and so off I went. Poor Granny: she's been sick at least twenty different times and in different parts of the empire during my short working career. The unbelievable thing was her timing; she was always unwell during the sales period, especially after Christmas and during the summer sales. But hey, you can't control such things. They were all happy, once I was back at the office, that she always recovered fully soon afterwards. If she only knew …

The following day, the alarm clock buzzed at

7.00 am and I was as ready to fight as I could be. Most importantly, I was ready not to disappoint my first real customer but to show her the path to enlightenment.

I arrived at her house at 8.30 am sharp, in the very best outfit I could put my hands on. Wow! I had to drive through a majestic, silver-birch-lined driveway and the sun was shining through the leaves, giving the trees a lovely glow. I parked in front of the two-storey, yellow-brick Georgian building and my eyes were sore from the opulence of the place. I could see on the far left side a beautiful lawn, perfectly mown, and further down a small lake. Lines of red and white roses were surrounding the main building. On the right was a triple garage and … stables. This place had stables as well? Or maybe they were the cats' mansions. If I wasn't allergic to cats, I could have asked her to adopt me … OH-MY-GOD! How could I forget about that? I had been so engrossed with the opportunity offered to me, by daydreaming of making fashion my way of living, that I had forgotten this minute, ickle, insignificant detail.

I was stuffed.

"Oh, my dear, please do come in." We shook hands and she invited me to follow. The lounge hosted at least twelve cats, but something told me "Lady Gaga" was not restricting all her little furry friends to that one room. For sure, there would be more upstairs, and in the kitchen and bathroom…

"Would you like a nice cup of tea, my dear? I've

put the kettle on …"

"That would be very nice of you, Miss Johnston." I looked around, hoping to find one of those tennis umpire chairs to put as much distance between her beloved creatures and myself as I possibly could, but there was none. That is a level of sophistication that interior designers have not reached yet, so I made a mental note of it.

"Oh, please – call me Marjorie; no need for formalities here. But please, sit down." She made a gesture towards a brown leather sofa that had more scratches than a Freddy Kruger victim and moved one of the five or six cats that were using it as a bed. A meow signalled that the cat was not amused by the sudden change of position. I braced myself and sat between a Persian and a Heinz with at least 65 different flavours of cat in it. Marjorie introduced the family, one by one, and off she went to the kitchen to prepare a cuppa.

Eighteen thousand pounds was not enough: not even close! Marjorie was in her mid-fifties, but she could easily have been seventy-five. She was wearing a pair of baggy dungarees and a red and pink flowery shirt. A straw garden hat was covering her curly, blond-white hair, which probably hadn't seen a hairdresser in the past twenty years, making her look like Uncle Jesse's British sister, straight out of *The Dukes of Hazzard*. I didn't dare imagine what was waiting for me in her wardrobe.

A cat was snuggling on my shoes, while another

one showed some interest in my Mulberry handbag at my side. Keep your claws off it, or I swear to God …

"Tea's ready, my dear." She served the beverage in a set of fabulous cups and … hang on … a Tiffany teapot in silver???? That was an exquisite item and, while I admit there are areas outside fashion that are complete black holes to me, I can recognise a piece of art when it's right under my nose. Maybe there was hope after all. I started looking around and, underneath the cats, there were indeed some nice pieces of furniture; they also kept some of them clean by means of their furry status. The paintings on the walls were not to my taste, mostly ancient stuff, but I could see that they also had some value. The only exceptions were a couple of abstracts down by the window, near the garden, that could have been reproductions of Kandinsky. I actually had the same poster in my bedroom years ago … hang on! Reproductions wouldn't fit well with Chippendale furniture and Tiffany teapots. Was it a test, or was it genuine? Help: am I getting the real measure of this woman???

"So, Griselda, tell me: what exactly is this consultancy of yours that Marianne keeps talking about?"

Hmmm, so she didn't know much of what I was trying to do? Interesting. Lucky me: I had my sales pitch ready.

"You see, Miss John … Marjorie, I'm a fashion

consultant. What I do is quite simple: I analyse people's wardrobes, the way they dress, and I give advice on how they could maximise their potential. My service will improve the way you look and … at-choo! … excuse me. Yeah … I was saying, by improving how you look I want to believe I can also improve your experience, both when you are shopping, so that you can remove your frustration when … at-choo! … excuse me, you buy clothes, and also make you look better when you're among your peers." A damn cat had just decided my lap was going to be its bed of choice, and it turned a couple of times before settling on me. Its tail was right under my nose, which instantly started itching.

"Oh, that sounds very interesting my dear. I think you might actually have a cold. If you want, I have a blanket here; it's quite clean, except that sometimes the cats sleep on it."

"That won't be necessary, Miss J … Marjorie. Shall we go and look at your wardrobe?" I tentatively suggested, hoping to get out as soon as I could.

"Very well, my dear; please follow me." She stood and made a gesture to follow her upstairs. When she reached the door she turned and addressed the cats "You be good boys and girls while Mommy goes upstairs, OK?"

A few of them decided to follow us. I prayed to God to save me.

CHAPTER 10

Mother couldn't believe I'd left the security of my secretarial job and a highly regarded nanny position with one of the best families in the neighbourhood to – how did she put it? –*pursue a dream*.

"GiGi, what is all this nonsense about being a fashion thing ... what did you call yourself?" she said on the phone.

"Fashion consultant, Mother."

"Yes, that was it. Listen, my dear, before you ruin your prospects altogether, you have to consider that you don't know anything about fashion."

"Excuse me?" Sometimes my mother has that

ability, surely a learned skill, to piss me off with the second sentence coming out of her mouth.

"There's a difference between shopping for yourself and getting paid for doing it on someone else's behalf."

"I know that; the difference is, first of all, that I get paid." I was already fuming. Why was she always trying to put me down; pick holes in everything I was doing? She did the same when I considered moving to France and I was still regretting it. And the other time I wanted to have a jet-ski business in Devon. OK, for the latter I didn't have any funds to start with, but that wasn't the point. What happened to '*Follow your dream, darling, as long as you're happy*'? When was it that that sentence went out of fashion? (Don't get me wrong, I love my mother; however, there have been plenty of times when I could easily have throttled her!)

"Don't patronise me, young lady. First of all, your taste might not be the same as someone else's," she continued. Brace yourself, GiGi, I thought; wear your helmet and wait for the cannon salvo. You won't get out of this conversation easily. For a moment I just thought of taking up the fight, just to have the excuse of hanging up the phone. "Do you remember last week when you came for dinner?"

Yeah … I did … what was her point? I asked her what she was getting at, knowing full well that she'd explain it to me whether I wanted her to or not.

"You were wearing blue and green. Don't you know that blue and green should never be seen? If you don't understand the basics, how could you even consider giving suggestions to others?" Except that she was referring to a JP Gaultier outfit that took ages to hunt down, and it was a piece of art.

"Mother, fashion evolves, as opposed to other things, or people who are still stuck in the Jurassic age."

"Watch your mouth, young lady; I'm still your mother." Now she was getting upset; she didn't like me reminding her that, occasionally, she should have refreshed her views and fully embraced the twenty-first century.

"Look, I do know what I'm doing. I have clear ideas and I'm good at this. Why don't you try to be supportive for once, instead of trying to pooh-pooh every idea I ever have?"

"I'm not doing that, GiGi; I'm just trying to be realistic. Use your common sense. It's risky starting a business from scratch and being self-employed."

Let's be honest: my mother takes pleasure in explaining how the world goes around, what was right (her view) and what was wrong (my view, for example), and everything has to conform to her way of seeing things. No room for negotiations there; it's like trying to have a discussion with the Prime Minister – not going to happen! She was on her second marriage and enjoying the money left to her by her father (that's even without taking into account her divorce settlement, as she was divorced at a time when blame was apportioned and so she received the larger share). Without having to worry about the day-to-day nitty-gritty, she could pontificate as much as she pleased.

I'm being unfair, I know; she's been a good mother, although careless at times. Well, my father disappeared many years ago with his secretary and she had to raise me, my brother and my sister single-handed; of course she would feel protective towards us. However, there comes a point in life when you have to let your offspring go, let them make their own decisions, even if they are the wrong ones, and let them learn from that. That's called life.

"Mom, this is something I want to do; so you can either be supportive, or we can close this conversation here, right now."

"Oh, OK: don't get upset, darling, I just wanted to avoid you being disappointed. It's a tough world, what with the recession and all …"

"I know, but I also think I have to do what I really want to, rather than keep a job just because it's the safe and secure option. I can go back to that anytime, if I fail."

"You have to think you won't be buying for yourself, if you really want to make it a success," she continued; but at least, by not mentioning my old job I knew she wasn't totally hostile to my ideas. I rather disagreed about that, though; I had to buy for my clients what I would like or, better, what I thought would be best for them. Leave them on their own, and they'd go back to buying the same old stuff. I had to be the catalyst to make them change, to embrace a new vision and, ultimately, become happier with themselves.

"How is Jordan, by the way?" Jordan was her second husband, or "the toy boy", as I used to call him. He knew that and on a few occasions we joked about it. He was twelve years younger than my mother and had a small firm building houses in the surrounding areas. He was actually quite funny and always glued to Google Maps, trying to find plots that could be suitable for building purposes. He would then approach the landowners – on occasion just people with a very large garden – and try to work out a deal, quite often successfully. I never asked why, at his young age, he stuck with my mother, but there was some sense in what he was doing. Apart from nagging me, Mother had a lot of interests and she was quite an interesting person, so I guess he got the better part of the deal. With the number of times he's told me that he makes every effort to stop my mother from nagging; however, I doubt he'll ever change that about her. I guess it's just a mother thing. Am I wrong on that?

Mom would have benefited as well from some of my consulting, to be honest, as she was going through phases. Occasionally she had very good taste, but at other times she could really scare me with her leopard-print leggings, or even her plain ones for that matter. It's also not as if she didn't know, as she'd mentioned it on many occasions, that I spend a lot of money on clothes and needed to curb that. I had to look good in my secretarial job, and even more so now, with my new venture taking shape. That didn't stop Mother, though. I was gobsmacked that during this conversation she hadn't brought up that pet subject of hers, about my spending, but she seemed to have resisted that urge – so far, at least.

"Oh, he's fine. He's almost finished building a set of terraced houses, and we're planning to go to the Caribbean after that, for a well-deserved vacation. "

Bummer! They never invited me when there was a "Caribbean" matter. Only for Christmas, to eat a chewy, dried-out turkey and carbonised potatoes. Mum hated cooking at the best of times, but she would never let Dad hire a cook or, unless it was a special occasion, go out to have a meal. I appreciated that she'd spent some time as a single mum, but, it wasn't as though she was hard up or anything like that.

"OK: have a nice vacation." I could have started listing the number of diseases you can get for overexposing yourself to the sun, suggesting all sorts of sun cream, just for the fun of hearing her nagging back. If they had some already, I could have suggested she bought a different brand, in the same way as Mom would have done if I was the one going away – but I resisted the urge. "Text me when you arrive, and send me a postcard. Have a lovely time."

"Will do, my dear. And be careful with that dream of yours; it isn't wise to leave something solid and secure, like your secretarial job, for an adventure. You know Uncle James did something like that and got burned when …"

"Mom! Gotta go. A client is calling. "It wasn't true. "Talk to you later."

"OK, but …"

"Bye!" and I hung up the phone. She could get on my nerves in a matter of minutes; perhaps she was doing some kind of training, as she was getting better and better at it. And I had to go back to my business.

CHAPTER 11

It's a difficult job, but someone has to do it. I mean, I needed to save Marjorie from herself and I had to use my utmost imagination if I had any chance of earning that huge amount of money. She seemed the type of person who would actually pay no matter what result I delivered, she was that nice; but the point I was trying to make was a different one. No matter how bad the clothes are, and despite the cats setting off my allergies, I felt I had to "really earn" that sum. I had to come out of those three or four weeks with pride and a feeling that I had deserved the job.

Not an easy task, nonetheless, but hey: if you want to achieve a result you have to work for it.

Success doesn't fall from trees.

Marjorie's wardrobe was – how should I say? – unusual. It was a decent one, if you were actually living in some rural area in the Dales, in the sixties. She would certainly have looked quite classy at the bovine market on Sunday, and for the Thursday quiz in the pub (still in the sixties, though. I hadn't checked, but I was sure they had moved on as well) – but in the twenty-first century in Berkshire she might look a bit outdated. OK – let's see. A fake Barbour from a garden centre in Bagshot: not my first choice. Another one, but this one was in blue rather than olive-green. A set of flannel shirts, squared almost tartan. "Marjorie, are you Scottish?" I had to ask. I was pretty sure that number of squares couldn't be associated in any way, shape or form with any of the most well-known Scottish clans (and if that was the case, tartan would be more than welcome), but perhaps some minor clan? Maybe a secret one.

"No, my dear: what a question. My family is right here from Berkshire, I believe at some point one of my great-grandfathers married an Irish lady, but I'm sure nobody after that even dared to do such a thing."

Near the pseudo-tartan shirts (a quick check revealed they were coming from the very same garden centre) – Ta-Daaa – was a very pretty collection of wellies. Of course they matched the coats: olive-green and blue. They were the top end, I should say – Hunter wellies – and I could also spot a few others. One pair had red flowers on them; there was a Christmassy pair in red with snowflakes and, of course, for the grand occasions, one pair with cats.

I'm being horrible, I know; poor Marjorie also had clothes that were more "regular", but there was nothing I was impressed with, nothing that would make her stand out from the crowd.

I had to spend a few days cataloguing the existing clothes and asking Marjorie how she ended up buying such outfits. It came out that, since the departure of her beloved husband a few years back, she'd decided to settle for "comfortable". She spent the first period of her life after her husband's death alone, not willing to see anybody or be involved in any kind of activity, despite all the efforts of her close friends and family. Eventually the requests and the invites became less frequent and she started dedicating more time to her cats: a couple at first, and then more and more, mostly from the nearby rescue centre in Old Ascot. The cats and her garden became her centres of attention, her reasons for living, mostly to fill her day and cover the pain she was still feeling for her departed husband.

I've never been in love in such a way, and I felt my heart sinking as her story was unveiled. She'd had a love that made her life happy, worth living and breathing, and made the two of them want to grow old together. They met when they were both in their mid-twenties and had never been separated since, not even for a short vacation. They were inseparable, two faces of the same medal; friends couldn't think about one without the other. The cancer had taken him almost a decade ago, and since then Marjorie had started her slow but inescapable decline. So, could I make any difference, with my little clothes advice and fashion tips on the tip of my tongue? Could I really transform Marjorie from an old cat lady into someone that could, again, enjoy the many years of life she had to come?

I had my doubts – some big ones, actually – that kept me awake at night. That, and my allergies, which made my nose become as big as a potato and as red as Father Christmas, despite the overdose of Benadril, corticosteroids, decongestant sprays, plus some other witch-doctor countermeasures I found from friends and family. I promised myself I would go beyond my capabilities to do what I could for Marjorie, and walk away without a penny if I couldn't make a difference.

I worked like a horse, early mornings at her house, showing her ideas I'd had the day before, and in the afternoon scavenging the most exclusive underground shops. I called in favours, made promises I couldn't maintain, just to come back to Marjorie with something suitable. We started getting somewhere and from being the nice girl who went to visit her for a chat, I became something different, something more. Perhaps a friend, I would say, despite being one permanently affected by allergies and with an odd fixation with clothes. We talked about our lives, our desires, the dreams we'd realised and the ones we hadn't. We laughed, we cried and we shared afternoon tea and cakes.

I was almost done with my work there. Marjorie got it: she perfectly understood what I was saying, not only about appearance, but also about the need for a human being to be out with others, especially one that loved us. To love, be loved and give the best of ourselves –even if sometimes the others are just cats.

I had a final surprise for Marjorie, when after six weeks (yes, I was late), she looked like an elderly model. I took her to my friend Mario, a hair stylist in Maidstone who could do wonders. Not that Marjorie needed them; she was an attractive woman still in her prime. It was just that the curly, white-blond hair was more suitable on a mop than on somebody's head. I was not disappointed; I can hardly describe the joy I found in her transforming into an even more beautiful woman than she already was. Her perplexed look soon transformed into a smile and then an even bigger one, as Mario proceeded with his work. She was happy and so was I.

The proof is in the pudding, or so they say, and for Marjorie it was in a dinner that Marianne had organised, involving most of the old "Lady Gaga's" friends. As soon as Marianne saw the results of my efforts (and maybe the result of my allergy), she looked me straight in the eye. There was no need to speak, and at that point, I knew from her expression that I could never go back to being a secretary. Also because they'd fired me the previous week for not showing up!

I knew I had a new career: something that was mine alone and that would make me happy going to work, every single day, for the rest of my life.

CHAPTER 12

We were ready to face Lady Whilsham, or at least, I was. Ritchie was shaking like a leaf and kept wandering around the office trying to figure out what he needed for the meeting. I teased him: "Ritchie, you have to do the bottoms-up approach in these situations."

"Oh, my beloved teacher, what would that be?"

"You start from the bottom and you go up, like a checklist. Do you wear shoes? Do you wear socks? And so on. Can't be unsuccessful."

"Ha ha: very funny. You say that because you've done it umpteen times. Presentation is everything; I have to have the right pad, the right pen. GiGi, this is a biggie; we can't fail."

"Don't worry; we're going to be fine. Just be yourself."

"I don't like myself at the moment, not until I find the right pen."

Eventually we were able to get out of the door and catch a taxi. And they say women take too long to get ready. Ha!

Fifteen minutes later we were in the Royal Borough of Kensington and Chelsea, where you could actually smell the richness even from within the taxi.

Lady Whilsham lived in an end-of-terrace in one of those little roads between Old Brompton Road and the Chelsea and Westminster Hospital; although I'm sure she wouldn't be amused if I called that beautiful three-storey house, with lovely cream bricks, an "end-of-terrace". A willow was growing in the front garden, and many other properties in the surrounding area were under renovation. For sure, they were digging underneath the properties – one of the latest fashions in that area. As space came at a premium and there were limitations on how much you could extend the properties, the very rich started expanding underground, sometimes even two or three levels, adding hidden garages, swimming pools and even cinema rooms.

The ones who hadn't quite got around to adding lower levels yet were constantly pissed off with their neighbours and their contractors, as the roads looked like a permanent building site.

We rang the bell and a butler (!) came to open the door; he didn't introduce himself, but he definitely looked like a Jarvis. The entrance hall was completely white, except for an oak staircase going to the upper floors. We followed Jarvis into the lounge, a room that could have easily swallowed my whole apartment and made it disappear. A beautiful oak floor was underneath us and the room was full of modern art – a painting here, a painting there, some sculptures on another side. We sat on one of the four cream sofas, looking towards the door so we could spot Lady Whilsham enter and not get caught off guard dreaming about a place like that. Ritchie kept moving his head from left to right, as if he was watching a tennis match or something, but then so was I.

"Yesss!" said Ritchie, "we struck the jackpot! GiGi, can you believe this house? I mean it must be worth twenty million. When I get rich I want a house like this, and a wedding in the garden."

Something was odd. I couldn't put my finger on it, but I had a gut feeling that a person with such a house surely couldn't really be too bad at dressing. There was still the possibility they could have hired an interior designer, splashed an awful amount of money to have this place done up. She was hiring us, anyway, so maybe … No, I was still not convinced; it was too perfect. The house had a personality; it exuded people with taste and clear ideas on what they wanted.

Any doubt disappeared once Lady Whilsham

appeared in the doorway. She was in her late-thirties and I couldn't fault her on anything. Perfect posture, perfect teeth, perfect hair and her clothes … ermm … I wish I could buy them – nothing to fault there either. What in hell's name were we doing here?

Ritchie was sitting at my side with his mouth open, starting to realise that if we had to improve the way she looked, we had a serious task on our hands – something that would require extensive planning and a lot (and I mean a LOT!) of research, scrapping all our usual suppliers and going to the top of the range. I mean, having to call stylists and have them work for us.

We stood and introduced ourselves; my mind was spinning trying to imagine how I could have pitched to her effectively.

Lady Whilsham was a Paula, and asked to be called by that name. She was confident, assertive and with clear ideas. I realised at that point that she owned the house, and she was definitely the one that had hand-picked all the items in here. It was Her taste.

"Lady … Paula: I'll keep it short. What are we doing here? You clearly don't need our services."

She smiled broadly and added, "May I offer you a cup of tea?" while signalling us to sit back on the sofa.

"That would be delightful," said Ritchie, who was starting to realise that our fortune was going to disappear like mist in the sun. That is, in some place warmer than London in the autumn. I had already budgeted for a set of Ferragamo shoes that, at this point, were shaking in their little boots and disappearing out of the window.

Jarvis probably had Vulcan ears, as he was nowhere to be seen, but appeared afterwards with a pot and three cups.

"Paula, what we do is …" I started my pitch, but with a light gesture of her hand, she made me shush.

"I don't need your help, as you can clearly see. But my daughter does."

The little Ferragamo shoes were still far away in the distance, but maybe not completely gone.

"Your daughter?"

"Indeed. I think she might have some of my husband's genes; after all. I have tried to educate her to the best of my ability and to her full potential, and that includes dressing properly – but I feel I've somehow failed in that task."

"How old is she?" asked Ritchie tentatively.

"Oh, she's just fourteen, and I'm sure it's a phase she's currently going through. The fact is, it seems that I'm unable to convince her to wear anything decent."

"What style of clothes is she wearing?" I enquired.

"I'm not sure about that, but she looks like a tramp." Paula was visibly upset; in her perfect life she also wanted a perfect teen, maybe forgetting that teens do what they do – most likely rebelling rather than conforming – but that I kept to myself. I wasn't letting anything out of my mouth until I'd assessed the situation better.

"Does she know we're here?" asked Ritchie, increasingly worried.

"Yes. She wasn't overenthusiastic about it, but I guess it won't take much to convince her."

Hmmm – now we had to convince a teenager to change her attire, as if that was an easy task. The advantage was, perhaps, that both Ritchie and I were not much older than her and maybe we could somehow connect with her.

"What's her name?" I asked, more to delay any further commitment than anything else. Ritchie started getting nervous and biting his nails, as he always does.

"She's called Henrietta, but you'll soon discover that she much prefers Harry, rather than Hettie, for reasons I can't really understand. "

"You know, we can't start phase one, which involves looking at her clothes, without her consent?" I urged. Trust was everything in our job and if we were to have the slightest chance of convincing "Harry" to change her ways, we needed to have her full approval and commitment. Rule one: admit you have a problem.

"Of course, my dear; that won't be a problem." I wasn't actually persuaded, but at that point what could I realistically do? We had to meet her before making a decision, before we could commit or walk away.

I looked around, hoping she would suddenly appear, maybe summoned by the Vulcan butler, Jarvis: but nothing happened. Paula spotted my anxiety and said, "Oh she isn't here at the moment, but she will be later in the evening. Would you mind coming back, let's say, around seven? We're having a party and she most likely won't take part. You could possibly go upstairs with her then and work something out."

"It'll be our pleasure, Madam," interjected Ritchie. Vulcan Jarvis suddenly appeared, and we knew our time was up.

CHAPTER 13

Ritchie and I ran back to the office, as we both kept a wardrobe there for emergency purposes. You never know when you'll need a change of dress; it might be a warm day and you need something fresher or, like this evening, you might be invited to one of the most prestigious addresses in London. OK, technically they hadn't invited us; we were supposed to go upstairs and convince good old Henrietta to shut up, give up whatever clothes she was wearing and make Mommy happy. However, I wasn't going to enter a house like that, at dinnertime, without being properly dressed and neither was Ritchie. Great minds think alike.

I picked up a red Valentino evening dress,

which I paired with cream and gold glitter peep-toe pumps and a matching clutch bag. Ritchie went for a double-breasted grey angora suit from Bottega Veneta, a pair of Kenzo ankle boots and a Kenzo shirt. He decided to button it up to the collar and not to wear a tie, a decision that I fully approved of. If he wasn't gay, I would have gone for him.

We were ready to go; it was time. We had great expectations from this job, despite the challenge Paula had put in front of us. Ritchie was still a bit nervous, it being his first time out to visit a client. He usually did the research work and kept in contact with the shops; however, he loved every minute of it. Good: we needed boots on the ground if we were to grow this business of ours.

We arrived on time in Kensington and parked behind a limousine; a very elegant couple climbed out and we waited until they had entered the house before knocking on the door ourselves. Better not to mix guests and employees (as we were). Vulcan Jarvis probably heard us arriving, as we had barely reached the door, not even touched the doorbell, when he opened the door. We sneaked in and had barely reached the stairs when a familiar voice called, "Griselda?"

I turned and there he was, good old Jasper, in evening dress, coming out of the lounge. "What are you doing here?!"

"Well, I'm working. Nice to meet you too, Jasper, I'm fine; thank you for asking."

"Oh. Yes, of course. I apologise." He looked

around and added "May I call you tomorrow? I think we started off on the wrong foot and … well, I would like to apologise."

I was still upset about the trick he'd pulled on Ritchie, but I had to admit he was gorgeous. Considering we were no longer in competition, despite his huge department store on my doorstep, I thought I should probably see him again. After all, I hadn't dated a real man in ages, probably six months, so what would be the harm? Let's not allow him to think I'd turned into a cold fish – and we'll see what happens.

"Sure: call the office in the morning and we can arrange something." Vulcan Jarvis was giving me killer looks, as I took the liberty of speaking to one of the guests – surely a capital sin in his mind.

"Will do." He hurried back into the lounge and, gosh, he had a nice bum. Why did his bottom inflate when I liked him and deflate when I was upset with him? Maybe he had one of those emotion sensor devices attached to it. I made a mental note to check at the first opportunity.

Jarvis coughed to bring some order into that unexpected event, and off we went upstairs to meet with Henrietta. Jarvis opened the door and announced us. Frankly I was expecting something more formal from him, like hitting a gong or the ringing of a bell to announce us: come on Jarvis – didn't they teach you anything? Anyway, Henrietta was lying on her bed, busy texting some friends or updating her status on Facebook.

"So, you're the fashion people who are supposed to sort me out?" she asked, not even looking, but immersed in whatever she was doing on her phone.

"Hmm … we are indeed the 'fashion people', but I can assure you we're not going to do anything that you won't agree to. And definitely we aren't here to sort you out."

"That's not what Mother said."

I was upset. No, I was furious. Years of hard work, and someone called us *to sort things out*? How dare she? Ritchie nudged me. He knew these were the sort of things that infuriated me.

"Let me explain how we work. We look at your wardrobe, we talk to you, and we give some suggestions on what to wear. That's it. If you want, we can help further in choosing the right attire, based on your tastes and personality. Or you can ignore what we have to say and carry on doing and wearing what you want. If you think you've found the perfect style for you and you're happy, we can call Vulcan Jarvis and we're out of your life."

"Who's Vulcan Jarvis?" she asked. For the first time she looked at us instead of her mobile. Ritchie started giggling.

"Ermm … well, I mean, we call the butler and off we go."

"Oh. Yes, I think Vulcan Jarvis sounds quite appropriate. Sometimes I also wonder if he's from this planet."

Now that I had her attention, albeit

involuntarily, I pressed on. "So, what do you think; shall we have a go? I promise it isn't going to be painful."

"I suppose so. I actually think it might be fun."

"Great. I'm GiGi and this is Ritchie." Keep the ball rolling, I thought, now that she's engaging; don't let her go.

"I'm Harry." She was a pretty girl, and showed signs of maturing into, probably, a stunning young woman. Lady Whilsham must have had her when she was very young. Or maybe she was adopted. I tried to see if I could spot any resemblance, but with all that heavy make-up, it would have been difficult.

"So, let's see. It seems you like vintage clothes." She was wearing a large, baggy male jacket, which she'd either got from her granddad or bought in some charity shop. The trousers were very tight and paired with fuchsia shoes that didn't go with anything else she had on. A flowery shirt was barely visible from underneath the jacket, as she was wearing a sort of bandana around her neck and a tartan scarf. It wasn't winter yet and I doubted Lady Whilsham was skimping on the heating bill, so it must have been some sort of fashion statement. Her long, dark hair was pinned at the nape.

"May we have a brief look at your wardrobe?" I asked, sensing that she wouldn't complain about that.

"Sure. Oh, the ones on the left are mine, and

those on the right are the ones Mom bought."

Something wasn't right. On the left side, Dirty Harry had a mishmash of clothes, some indeed vintage, others not – regular T-shirts, coloured items. I couldn't see any pattern in what she was buying, nor a rationale that would bring them together. It seemed like a hoarder's wardrobe where she stored different things, maybe worn randomly. The right-hand side didn't catch our attention; imagine what a rich mom with an attitude for perfection would buy, and there you were. Nice, but boring; for Harry, at least.

Ritchie was also perplexed. "Could you tell me more about this vintage thing? I mean, it doesn't seem you have much old stuff in here. Is it a new thing?" he asked her.

"No, that's just to piss off my mother."

Both Ritchie and I burst out laughing. Indeed, both of us understood where she was coming from, especially considering Lady Whilsham's quest for perfection. That seemed to break the ice a little among us. "So you're not really into vintage clothes?" he pressed.

"I don't think so. As I said, it's to piss off my mother. And to be unique, I suppose."

"We've all been there, darling." Ritchie was in his element; he was enjoying every minute of it, considering his past.

"Which one of the two is more important to you?" He was doing great, so no point in me interrupting, just to ask the very same questions.

"I suppose being unique. I rather want people to notice me, not being like everybody else. We all wear uniform at school, so when I'm out I want people to talk about me, comment; give me attention, I mean."

"OK, I think I get the point." Ritchie opened his bag and fired up his laptop. A minute later, he was sitting at the desk with Harry discussing a couple of ideas.

"You see, this is a quite new Scottish designer, I was thinking you might like something like that, perhaps?"

"Hmmm …"

"And for example you could have those other couple of items that match with that shirt?" He was showing a pair of skinny jeans and T-shirts from House of Holland, plus some other dresses. He briefly switched to Bregazzi and my heart sank: *Come on, don't you dare move on; stay on that damn page and put it all together …*

Ritchie didn't disappoint me. He knew what he was doing and how to strike the right chords. He was taking care of the customer rather than the purchaser.

"Oh, I think I get what you mean. I think that would actually piss off my mother even further."

"Darling, let's not forget your mom is footing the bill. Our point is that you can build a style without being trashy."

It was almost nine in the evening and it was getting late. The host didn't even bother to ask if we were hungry. "Harry, have you eaten already?"

"Yes, I had dinner early, as there were all those guests and I didn't want to mix with them. You know, all those stories on how tall I've become … I hate it."

"Well, we've pretty much finished our exploration. So if you're interested, would you be so kind as to let your mother know?"

"Oh yes." She seemed excited to have us around, giving advice that was more suitable for her age. Maybe we had a chance to make another customer happy. "I'll definitely tell her you convinced me." She had a nasty grin on her face and we braced ourselves. Our job can be tricky at times.

She pushed a button near the phone and Vulcan Jarvis teleported himself to the door. It was time to leave.

CHAPTER 14

The contract from Lady Whilsham arrived by fax just as I was supposed to be going out for lunch with Jasper. We classified her as a Gold client, as we had serious doubts that Lady Mummy (Whilsham) would allow Harry a decent budget. In addition, she'd decided she would pay for the clothes directly, so our earnings would come only from consultancy. Despite the thirty-million-pound mansion (or was it twenty million as I guessed earlier?), she bartered on the price as if we were stealing her last pennies. We had to start the following day.

Meanwhile, Ritchie started his nagging dance around me, trying to get me to reconsider that offer from Jasper. He had mentioned it a couple of times previously and each time I had dismissed his remarks. That frustrated him even further, because it was obvious in his mind that we could accomplish more from within a large organisation, not forgetting also that we would finally have had a decent salary to live on, rather than keep scraping the barrel or reinvesting in the company. That is, when we weren't *investing* in our own wardrobes. The bank wasn't particularly happy about our line of business; sometimes they didn't get what we were doing, and when they did understand, we were right in the middle of a crisis and the numbers didn't look good.

That morning Ritchie was on a mission, thinking I would change my mind. "Drop it, Ritchie. It's just a date."

"I've never questioned you, GiGi – ever, ever, ever before. But this time you're making a big mistake." No, I was not …

"I told you, we'd be simple employees. They'll squeeze us like a lemon and as soon as they don't need us any more: thank you very much, here's your statutory redundancy pay and off you go". And even, probably, forget to thank us for our service.

"You don't know that's what's going to happen. If they want us, they have their reasons." Well, they want me, dear friend; but they made it quite clear you're out of the picture. They don't see in you what I see – your friendship, your dedication and your passion. Why don't you let it go, Ritchie? Do me a favour and let it go. We already have troubles; we can't afford any more. If he only knew how many times I hadn't taken my salary just to be able to afford his. How many times I'd had to sell my most precious possessions on Ebay to keep us afloat, begging for favours and pushing some old customers to meet payment deadlines.

"Look. I don't really want to talk about it any more. I have a date to get to."

"Fine."

It wasn't fine, if I knew him as well as I thought I did. Probably he would bite his nails until they hurt, buy himself something expensive and then most likely regret it – a feeling that I knew only too well, and which had got me into trouble on more than one occasion. But what could I have done? Pitch Ritchie to Jasper?? We were friends, after all, so why not?

I left the office and left him at his desk, with his anger mounting, and me feeling bad for not telling him the truth.

This time Jasper had chosen a restaurant in a nice location just by the River Thames, elegant but not sumptuous, which I was glad about. He was already seated at a table by the window and he stood as soon as I entered. We'd exchanged a couple of emails since we met at Lady Whilsham's house, but we kept it flirty and light. I didn't ask questions and he didn't volunteer answers.

We kissed on the cheek and sat down.

"How's business?" he asked, as his first question. I was wondering if I was the only one thinking about this lunch as a possible date.

"Doing OK: how's your mall?" I fired back. That put him in his place; he probably wouldn't like to hear me saying that, calling it a mall, but I didn't start the war, after all.

"Hmmm … doing fine; we should open in a couple of weeks."

"Did you find your store manager eventually?"

"Actually yes, but if you've changed your mind, we're still in time to sort things out," he added, with a bit of hope in his voice.

"Did you change your mind about Ritchie?" I enquired. I had to know.

"No."

"You should reconsider; he's very talented." I went on describing how he was now part of the firm, how well he was doing in managing the old accounts and how he was also learning about getting new customers. It was as if all my words were lost in the wind.

"Maybe, but as I said there's no place for him at this point." He was firm; no sign of doubt.

"Well, then we don't have a deal." That sealed it; I would never bring up the matter again. It was becoming humiliating having to beg for a job, even if it wasn't mine, strictly speaking.

"You're working for Paula now?"

"She's paying the bill; her daughter's the customer."

"Harry?" He looked surprised. "That's very strange indeed. What's wrong – don't you like the vintage style?"

"I love it; I just think it needed a bit of tweaking and guidance."

"Is Paula OK with that?" He seemed over-interested in what we were doing with Harry.

"I don't know; she isn't the customer – Harry is. Paula's just footing the bill. You seem to know them very well." There was something strange in his look: I could feel it.

"I do. Harry is my daughter and Paula's my ex-wife."

W-H-A-T?

Well, we had never actually spoken about our private lives before. The previous meeting had been a business one, and even in the emails we exchanged later we were busier flirting rather than exchanging life details. I didn't know if I was upset or not. OK, I hadn't asked, but who's going to ask on a first date, "Are you by any chance the father of my latest client?"

I was thirty-one (although I prefer thinking I am a 28C) and had never had a child of my own. I had thought about it many times, but I'd actually never found the right partner – the one who gives you butterflies in your stomach, makes you have "the hots", makes your mineral water sparkle … well, *the* one. Jasper not only had a daughter; she was a teen. It seemed a bit of a bombshell at that moment, but Harry was a nice girl and I think we had established a good relationship … Hang on, GiGi: this is a first date, don't forget, so leave the kids, grandkids and wedding plans out, until at least the third date.

"Oh, I didn't notice the resemblance, but actually I wasn't looking for one. How did that happen? … well, not how did that happen … I mean, you must have been very young."

"I was. We were both in our twenties and Harry came as a surprise." He seemed fine to talk about it, of which I was glad. Nothing kills a first date like the children talk. "When that happened, the only thing we could think of was our daughter, despite all the pressure we had from our families."

"They didn't support you?" I enquired

"Both families had interests at stake. The Whilshams are an old family, but had no money, while mine had money but few connections in the upper crust. They wanted something different for us."

"And you didn't?" I pressed as the story was becoming interesting.

"Paula was sitting on the fence, at the beginning. Later she started regretting we'd had Henrietta and made a point of making my life miserable. In her opinion she'd wasted the best years of her life and wouldn't ever forgive me. Nonetheless, she fought for custody and she won. Plus she received a hefty injection of cash from the divorce."

"How long ago was that?"

"About five years ago. Now I can see Harry as

much as I want, as long as I keep paying." Jasper was genuinely sad about the whole situation, and besides our disparities of opinion in the world of fashion, he was a great person. I could see the spark in his eyes every time he mentioned Henrietta.

"What about you? How did you start your career? I'm actually curious."

I told him my story, which was far less exciting.

CHAPTER 15

The money I earned from Marjorie, despite being a considerable amount, didn't last me very long. I thought I was in business, but the reality was I had just got lucky. Like the majority of twenty-odd-year-olds in this country, my business skills were not good at all and I was still spending more than I could afford. It was a sort of euphoria that caught me, the kind that someone might experience as a young person when she finally wins the lottery. You start planning, trying to be sensible but inevitably it drags you into a spiral of spending and easy life and, sooner than you expect, you're left with nothing.

Life was easy.

At that time I had a boyfriend, Martin. We'd been together for almost a couple of years, and I was in love with him. He had everything. He was tall, handsome, with dark curly hair and a juicy bum. Blimey, he should have been an actor. The problem was that I wasn't the only one noticing the package and swarming around him, but worse than all that was that he knew it. He was indeed self-aware of his status and – how should I say? – sometimes he slipped into bad habits that didn't make him so perfect after all. The bastard was a cheater.

I didn't realise it until it was too late: far too late to do anything about it.

Yes, I was in love and I thought Martin would be the right counterpart for me – the person I could live the rest of my life with. He was caring, affectionate, with the right amount of scoundrel in him to fascinate me. I met him for the first time at a party organised by Helena for her birthday; her parents were away and she got permission to use the house and invite some friends. I'd been staying with her since the previous evening and when the alarm clock buzzed at eight o'clock sharp, we jumped out of bed ready to prepare the necessary. We could have made our life much easier by getting everything from a shop, but we were proud people and wanted to make the effort ourselves. Where's the fun, otherwise?

As these things go, we spent the morning "planning", which translated into having even less of a clear idea by lunchtime. Something needed to be done, and quickly, in order to avoid a catastrophe. A few phone calls were made and, as if by a miracle, Adam appeared with a bunch of music records that he would arrange that very afternoon, Jasmine was in charge of the decorations, Ritchie, Rebecca and Paul were in charge of getting the beverages, or booze, as someone kept referring to it.

Helena kept the task of organising matters (two leaders accomplish nothing) and I was in charge of cooking. Nibbles are the most challenging task; we were going to have at least twenty people – I correct myself, twenty wolves – and ensuring there was enough for everybody wasn't an easy undertaking. My only hope was that Paul would take the lead on the booze expedition, which he did, coming back with a significant catch.

By the time I'd put the cakes in the oven I was covered in flour, had egg marks all over me and resembled the surviving victim of a bakery explosion. It was at that point that Helena shouted, "GiGi, could you please get the door?"

The guests weren't due for another hour; maybe some more help was arriving? I ran to the door and BANG! – there he was: Martin, looking at me in that pitiful state.

"Hmm, can I help you?" Whoever that guy in front of me was, at that point I was silently cursing Helena for asking me to attend to the door. Come off it – I hadn't even thought of making myself presentable.

"Yeah, I'm Martin; I'm here for the party."

"Oh … yes … sure. Come on in. You're a bit early." Helena, you are dead. If I only knew a guy like that was coming, like hell would I have agreed to even enter the kitchen. Once inside, I did my best Houdini act and disappeared upstairs to get ready.

It is the "love at first sight" that gets us into trouble. That very first impression we have of someone, which makes your imagination run free and clouds your judgment. Never, ever, ever believe in love at first sight. If you are tempted, run! Even if you're even thinking about it, run! My gut feeling told me that Martin would be trouble, but I did my level best to ignore it and I got hurt, badly.

At the beginning, it was love.

I'd gained another couple of new customers after Marjorie and things were going decently. I could afford nice clothes, going out, having fun – you know, everything one needs at that age, and I had a gorgeous boyfriend. I loved him to pieces and although in some aspects of our lives we didn't really get along, I thought that time would settle the matter – knowing each other, smoothing some corners and making some tiny compromises for the sake of the couple. So what, if he wasn't interested in going shopping with me? We had our own little space, periods of time that each of us could dedicate to him- or herself. The rest was like being in paradise: a job that I loved and a partner I treasured. Yeah, there was that little annoying matter of his mobile phone – always glued to it and secretive with it – the football with friends and the occasional poker night. But who doesn't have peculiarity in life? So when he asked if we should live together I was over the moon and didn't think twice about it. Soon afterwards, a proposal would come, for sure, and then we could get married.

We started thinking big; I mean, why rent and pay someone else's mortgage when we could have our own place? So we eventually decided that having our own house was the way to go, maybe starting with a two-bedroom place, and later seeing how it went. The little details about the mortgage were soon bypassed; although I had a decent salary from my job as a fashion consultant, it became extremely difficult to demonstrate that I had a regular income. The bank manager thought my business was a bit erratic, inconsistent, and they would have expected far more customers than I had at that point in time. Martin and I decided (but maybe it was his idea) that we could arrange things differently, I would provide the deposit and he would make the monthly mortgage payments. It seemed fair to me at that point in time and therefore I parted with half of my capital, ready to invest in this new adventure.

The fact is, if you put down the deposit but don't have your name on the deeds, you own nothing, and that was the situation I was left in when one evening I caught him cheating on me. It was supposed to be a poker night, so I went out with some friends, only to catch him snogging with a brunette dressed like a tart. Mum would have said "I told you so," had she even known about that one.

I was livid. We spent days discussing the matter, I cried a river bigger than Michael Bublé's one, but when eventually he told me that men "had needs", that sealed it. Martin was out of my life for ever. What kind of sentence is that? Women have needs too, and the first is having their boyfriends not cheat on them.

I packed my things, loaded the boot of my car and off I went. I didn't get that far though, because at the second set of traffic lights I was flooding; tears were running down my cheeks and I could barely see the road. I parked on the kerb and stayed there for what seemed an eternity, sobbing and repeating to myself how foolish I had been.

I had no place to go: I was homeless. Going back to my parents wasn't an option, not after I'd quit my job and decided to be self-employed. A wave of "I told you so" was waiting for me there, and being at my parents' place would only remind me of my failures, how silly I was. I made a couple of phone calls, but I hit a brick wall; then I suddenly remembered that Ritchie was back from Paris, where he had spent the previous six months. I knew he didn't have a partner these days, so maybe I could crash on his sofa for a couple of days until I was back on my feet.

The phone rang six times before he picked up and I could hear his reassuring voice. "Darling, are you OK? It's two in the morning."

"I broke up with Martin" I sobbed, "I left him. He was cheating on me."

"I thought he wasn't the right guy for you. Where are you now?" He was calm and reassuring: finally, someone I could trust, at least to explain how I was feeling.

"I don't know. I'm in my car somewhere near Winkfield. I don't know what to do next." I felt completely lost, parked in a car full to the brim with clothes and unable to think.

"Can you drive?" he asked "Otherwise I'll come and get you."

"Yes, I can drive."

"Good, darling. Well, you know where I live; there'll be a warm cuppa waiting for you when you arrive."

I loved Ritchie; there wasn't any need to explain to him – he knew when words were useless and it was time to do something.

"Thank you, Ritchie. I really appreciate it."

"Don't mention it, sweetheart. See you soon."

And off I went, heading towards Windsor, to my dear friend Ritchie. I ended up spending more than a few months at his place, and he didn't complain once. At some point I was really depressed and starting overspending; I don't know exactly why, but I guess I was trying to compensate for my loss, trying to cheer myself up a bit. But things went too far and thank God Ritchie was around. He acted like a therapist and a true friend, in not only listening to my sob story and comforting me during those months, but also in stopping me from ruining my life and in helping me to regain control of my finances before I became completely broke. He liked his share of spending, but at that point he became my guardian angel, making me realise I shouldn't be wasting my life, losing myself in the depths of despair. He picked up the pieces, one by one, and managed to put them back together. He never left me alone for one moment and made me realise there were things worth living for –friendship, for example. I will always be grateful to Ritchie for what he did for me in that dark period of my life. When he lost his job at Jaeger's two years later, I didn't think twice about giving him a position in my firm and sharing with him the good, the bad and the ugly. Nothing would separate our friendship in the future. Or so I thought.

CHAPTER 16

Things were going great guns with Harry. We took her out shopping many times and thanks to her mother's allowance, it was an easy task to complete her wardrobe. I had started populating the clothes-matching program a few days before and it would be ready by the end of the week. Usually this was a task Ritchie would do, but this engagement was his party, so I took most of the grunt work on my shoulders. It was at the point when I had actually put a complex item into it, a dress with multiple colours and shades, that it hit me. People don't go around with computers or, at least, not all the time; but they do indeed go around with mobile phones, and nowadays you have all sorts of Apps. Why not have a GiGi App? No more lengthy typing: just take pictures, add a few tags and the job would be done. I knew it was a bit more complex than that – I mean, the program should be able to let you scroll among all the items with a certain tag – but imagine! You're in a shop, you take a snap of the dress you like (or shoes, or scarf – the possibilities were endless) and the app would show you all the things you have in your wardrobe that match it. No more describing style, length, colour, designer, but having all your clothes at your fingertips: that's technology.

Of course, neither Ritchie nor I would know where to start, to develop such a thing, but programmers were available all over the place, so it was a matter of just finding the guy with the right skills to do it. Proud of my idea, I thought we could fund it when we received our money from the Harry assignment, maybe giving it free to our customers and charging others for using it, or something like that. I hadn't spoken about it to Ritchie yet, but was sure he would love it.

Harry was increasingly satisfied with the results, as we were keeping her style but making it more consistent and less tatty. She was a diamond in the rough, grasping the basic concepts I was explaining to her, and soon she would be able to continue by herself. Hell, in a few years this girl could even become my boss. What was more important was that she trusted us, knowing we were trying to do something, as simple as it was, to improve her life. With appearance, as I know very well, occasionally there is a fine line between being picked on for the wrong reasons rather than for the right one.

We also started discussing other matters, such as school, boyfriends, family relationships, and how difficult it was being a teenager. Both Ritchie and I felt very sympathetic to her and, on more than one occasion, we looked each other in the eye and started laughing. "What's happening? What did I say?" Harry would enquire and we would explain to her that we'd both been there. Ritchie usually was the one spitting out the anecdotes, from both of us, while I was slightly more reserved.

Eventually I had to tell her that her father was a person of interest and I was dating him. That didn't seem to upset her. On the contrary, she proposed that one day we should hang out together. We actually met her father on a couple of occasions and she received his thumbs-up on the new style, which made her extremely happy.

A couple of weeks down the line, Lady Inquisitive caught Ritchie on the stairs and asked how things were progressing, and when she'd be able to see some results. The little coward didn't have the heart to tell her that actually we'd already passed the initial stage and Harry had been wearing the new outfits for a week. We needed to do something, so we regrouped in one of the rooms upstairs and worked out a plan.

"It's not going to be easy," said Harry. "The FOP

will hate everything with her guts."

"Not necessarily," I added. "Maybe if we present the work in the right way, introduce your new style to her in the right way, she might not like it, but at least she won't complain too much."

I needed to see Lady "PainInTheNeck" as soon as possible and face her. Where is Vulcan Jarvis when you need him to appear? I went downstairs and knocked on her studio door. Lady Busy was at the computer and flicking through papers when I entered. What she was doing was a mystery: she didn't have a job – blimey, she'd never had to earn a living in her entire life – but nonetheless she made her best impression of a multinational CEO.

"Ermm … I was wondering if you'd have time this afternoon to see the results of our work."

"I'd be delighted," said Lady Expectancy. "GiGi, maybe you have a few minutes to spare? I'm going through these invoices, and I see you've worked hard to get a new wardrobe for Henrietta."

"We have indeed, and she loves it," I cautiously added, as something seemed to be bothering her.

"About that: there are a number of names on these invoices that I don't recognise. Kane, Bregazzi, Holland … what happened to the famous designers such as Valentino, Versace and so on?"

How could I have explained to her? Harry was a teen and sometimes what is good for the mother is not necessarily good for the daughter. Henrietta needed to find her own style; at that age individuality was everything.

"Maybe we can show you something later on, in the afternoon?"

"What about now?" asked Lady Nosey.

"Sure, why not? Here or in the lounge?"

"Let's do it in the lounge."

"OK," I said, "give us a few minutes to get ready."

I ran upstairs and the news didn't go down well. Ritchie started pulling together clothes, running left, right and centre, pulling out shoes and then discarding them. Harry was on her bed, texting or Facebooking and barely paying any attention to our efforts. "She's gonna hate it," she said in a very flat voice, without diverting her eyes from the phone.

"OK, here's the plan. Ritchie, you choose the first outfit; I'll sit in the lounge with Paula and give her an introduction. Then Harry comes in, OK?"

"Roger that."

Come on, Griselda – you can do it! I'd had some difficult customers in the past and on occasion I went a bit wild, but I knew what I was doing. Eventually, they understood what I was proposing to them and appreciated it; why should this be any different?

I gave the news to the team and off we went downstairs, ready for the show. I sat on the sofa near Lady Impatient and started describing the approach I had followed, building from Harry's previous attire and … and she stopped me mid-sentence, showing me the palm of her hand.

"Whenever you're ready, guys," I said from where I was, maybe a bit louder than I wanted. I could hear them getting ready, and ta-da … here was Harry in her fabulous new look.

Lady Incredulity looked at her walking into the room and kept moving her head left and right, as if she was observing an imaginary Ping Pong match – or maybe because she was disapproving. She turned toward me and said, "Is this a joke?"

"No, Madam, I assure you it is not."

Lady PissedOff was not amused: not one bit. She jumped to her feet and started saying this was outrageous; we had spent an awful amount of money to transform her daughter into an unpresentable kid; she would not tolerate being ridiculed by her friends over this. I tried to interject, but she stopped me again. I started getting annoyed.

It was at that point that Harry interjected. Still looking at her phone, she said, "Dad seemed to like it."

"You mean that you lot showed this to my ex-husband before I had seen it? How dare you!"

"GiGi is dating him, so why not?" added the little snake, her eyes still on the phone, probably tweeting her mother's rant as she spoke. I quite liked her; she had personality.

But that sealed it; Vulcan Jarvis suddenly appeared and accompanied us to the door. From the lounge we could still hear her screaming, "… never pay them for this eyesore…" and then,

"They'll never find another job, I promise."
It was time to leave.

CHAPTER 17

"What just happened?" asked Ritchie as soon as the door had closed behind us.

"Beats me," I answered, "Lady Complacent seemed ecstatic at our work, and then suddenly she changed her mind. Must have been the tea."

"GiGi, this is no time for jokes. If she really isn't going to pay us …"

"I don't think she'll go that far. Come on, we did a great job, Harry loves us to pieces; she's going to be a star among her friends."

Ritchie was far from convinced, or I should say, he was panicking. "GiGi, if we don't get that money … I need it. I have rent to pay."

"Give her a day or two; she'll come to her

senses." I wasn't convinced and I even sounded false when I heard my own voice saying it. But, what could I do? We had done the right thing; we'd stuck to our principles, right?

The phone rang; it was Jasper. "GiGi, what have you done?"

"Good news travels fast, doesn't it?" Ritchie was giving me looks, so I mouthed "Jasper".

"Harry called me. She's thrilled, but I'm not sure whether that's because of your work or because you upset Paula."

"Can one go without the other?"

"You have to tread carefully, GiGi, Paula can be a powerful enemy." Ritchie, in the meantime, was doing his best impression of a landing signal officer, moving his arms up and down trying to catch my attention.

"I'm sure she'll understand, in a day or two." But I was far from being sure.

Ask him to take us! We need a job! Ritchie was miming; I turned to look the other way.

"I wouldn't be so sure. She can be a frightful bitch when she wants."

"OK, I got it. What should I do?" I asked, Ritchie was panicking and started poking me on the shoulder to get my attention.

"If she's as upset as I think she is, run and hide. She'll do everything she can to ruin your career. I think she knows some of your customers as well, right?" There was a sense of urgency in Jasper's voice, as if he was really worried about what could happen.

"She's not going to put a bounty on my head, is she?" I tried to ease off the feeling that I was in big trouble, but I wasn't able to convince myself, let alone anyone else.

"GiGi, you know how these things work. Word of mouth, and if you've upset someone like Paula, you're doomed. She's got all the right connections." It was official. I was stuffed.

"OK – let me think about something and I'll call you back, all right?"

"Sure. Catch you later. I also have to go; we're opening soon. You sure you don't want to come and work for me?"

"Same conditions as before?"

"You got it."

"No thanks."

I didn't know whether I liked him more or whether I hated him. On the one side I was attracted to him, and even his refusal to accept Ritchie, although upsetting, made sense. I would have done the exact same thing if I didn't believe in someone. Shame: he was wrong about my partner, but at least he had demonstrated integrity. So how was I going to face that problem? We needed to tread carefully. I ended the call and urged Ritchie to come back to the office with me. Maybe we could sort out something or work on a plan.

Unfortunately, when we reached the office we were both drained by the experience and it was all we could do to sit on the sofa, looking at our feet and wallowing in our misery. For a long time we sat there without saying a word; there wasn't much to be said, to be honest. We needed that job to survive, and without it everything would be so much more difficult. I had some savings I'd put aside for rainy days (at Ritchie's suggestion, after my credit-card issues), but it was far too little. Oh my God, was this the end of it?

"What if we give the money back? – I mean, what she's spent on Harry's clothes? In that way, even if she didn't like our job, she can't really complain, can she?" I thought about that unexpectedly, without even thinking about the consequences, but it was the right thing to do, even if we had to tighten the crocodile belt a bit more.

"Darling, did you see the final bill? That was an outright shopping spree, almost fifteen grand. We don't have that kind of money." There was panic in his voice; if there was one thing he hated, it was being without money. Especially now that he had a new boyfriend and he needed to show off a bit. Who liked to appear a loser?

I had to put it right, no matter what our situation. "Listen, I'm going to call her and explain we are refunding her what we've spent." At that point I received a text message. It was from Harry.

"Luv the new look. Boys around like flies on honey. Its gr8. Party wth gfs l8r, gotta go. X x x Harry. P.S. 10x LY4E." It was nice to see that at least someone appreciated our efforts, although it didn't make any difference to our situation.

"Why don't we take that offer from Jasper? Maybe we're still in time. You know they open next week."

"Ritchie, I told you: that's not an option." How can you possibly love a man, then hate him with all your guts, then love him again and after ten minutes want to kill him? That was how my feelings for Jasper kept swinging. And don't tell him I mentioned the L-word; he doesn't know it yet. Gee, I don't know it either, so please keep your mouth shut for the moment until I can get a clearer idea, OK?

"You can be so stubborn, GiGi. Come on, let's do it. Even if we have to repay the bitch, with those salaries we could do it in no time at all."

"Ritchie, will you stop nagging on that point? I said no!"

"Oh, now I'm a nag." He was upset. "After all these years I'm becoming a nag. Well, darling, it must be the age, right?"

"Ritchie …"

"Come on, be honest: tell me that I screwed up my first job and now we're in trouble; that it's all my fault." That was unexpected; how could he possibly think I was blaming him? That was unfair; after all, we worked as a team and I'd been amazed by how well he'd handled Harry. He possibly had done a better job than I could have; he not only really connected with her and found his way in, but he also chose the right items to complete her look and made it seem effortless. It took me ages to reach that level of confidence. Ritchie was a natural and, given a few years, he'd become better than I am.

"Oh, don't bother. I'm going for a walk." He got up out of his seat and walked out of the door. He was frustrated, but what had happened wasn't his fault. We all get nervous when money is tight and in his position, maybe planning something more with his boyfriend, I don't know if I would have acted any differently.

I braced myself for the worst and called Lady Whilsham to tell her the news. Vulcan Jarvis kept me on hold for what seemed a geological period and then connected me through. I explained the plan to refund all the expenses she had sustained for Harry; the girl and her mother could keep everything they might think suitable and I would collect the rest. Let them sort out what; I was exhausted and frankly, although I was sympathetic towards Harry, I couldn't possibly judge or intrude on their relationship. I also negotiated to have three weeks to pay back the whole amount – the first instalment immediately, and the rest during the following three-week period. After a few words like "unacceptable", "disgusted", "unsatisfactory" and "deplorable", we had an agreement that I would formalise it in a letter to her. There was still the question of my reputation. However, if Lady Whilsham wanted to slander my name there was nothing I could do about that. Go ahead, Lady Bitch: do what you have to do. Now that we'd agreed on refunding her costs I could at least sleep at night.

I opened the computer and started listing all my possessions at a cut-down price on eBay, I needed money fast if I was to have a chance of repaying the debt and pay Ritchie's salary as well. Asking the bank for a loan was not an option.

In the past few months that had become a habit. Gosh, maybe I should have kept working as a secretary and forgotten about the rest, or started a career in the delivery business. With all the eBay stuff I shipped, I had the experience.

The first repayment went out a couple of days later, after I had raided my bank account, the sugar jar with the emergency funds and pawned some of my jewellery. Ritchie didn't show up, having his boyfriend call in sick on his behalf. Things were looking grim.

CHAPTER 18

"What do you mean, they didn't pay you?" Mother asked.

"Her mother didn't appreciate our work. We're exposed for fifteen thousand pounds." I briefly explained the whole situation to her.

"But the girl, that Harry – she liked the work?"

"Yes, but that hardly counts, as it's the mother forking out the money."

"I told you that business model where you have to pay upfront for the clothes was risky." Here she comes: I knew she was going there – blame me instead of taking my side. We didn't do that for everybody, only those where we had a good chance of charging higher prices. Lady Whilsham seemed the right candidate.

"I know. We discussed that, Ritchie and I, and it was worth a shot. She could have opened an awful lot of doors for us."

"Are you going through solicitors?" she asked after a pause, "Because we have some family friends …"

"No, Mother. Taking them to court will cost money that we don't have and it might ruin our reputation. Would you work with someone that takes clients to court?"

"I wouldn't work with a fashion consultant in the first place." she retorted. "All that nonsense about telling people what they should wear."

"Mother, we talked about that …" – but I couldn't finish my sentence. She was already on a mission.

"And the fact that you moved to London; I bet you're spending thousands in rent alone."

I was, but that wasn't the point. We needed to be in London to attract the rich clients, to be visible. We had overstretched ourselves, but it was the right thing to do. I only hoped she wouldn't go into "Finance one-o-one" mode and explain to me what I should have done.

"GiGi, why do you keep insisting on working for yourself in that business? You work so hard and after all this time, you're still struggling. You have to have an exit strategy. Maybe you could go back to doing your secretarial work until the economy picks up."

"Mom, I would never do that. I wouldn't work for someone else any more."

"Yes, but you're overloaded and have debts. You don't have time to do anything with your life. How are you ever going to have a family if you keep doing things like that?"

I knew where she was going; she wanted to be a grandmother. My sister was too young, my brother was too busy enjoying himself to ever think about settling down, and that left me as the only appropriate candidate.

"Mum, don't start again on the family matter; when the time is right, it'll happen."

"That's what your Auntie Gina kept saying. She was so engrossed in her work, and now she's alone. You don't want to end up like Auntie Gina, do you?"

I remembered the story too well; she was a sort of black sheep in the family. She had decided to import wines and groceries from Italy to the UK. At first she sold door to door, but then started approaching restaurants and eventually she set up her own shop in London. She specialised in products from the Emilia Romagna: hams, all sort of salamis and wines typical of that region but that were unavailable in this country. She made a fortune and actually, she was a hero of mine. The fact that she never married or had any children was not accepted well by my relatives. On the contrary, I thought she lived the life she wanted, but I didn't say that to my mother. Did I want to end up like

Auntie Gina? I wouldn't have minded it.

"As I've said many times, Mother, when the time is right and I've found the right person, I'll consider that."

"Just don't wait too long. You'll be old and full of wrinkles and you won't even realise it until it's too late."

Yeah, the wrinkle matter. That was a favourite subject of hers. Why was she so obsessed with it?

"I'll put some cream on, OK?"

"Now don't be sarcastic with me, young lady. In a few years' time you'll appreciate what I'm saying," she continued, "Are you moving away from London, at least? To some place cheaper?"

"We haven't decided yet … most likely not," I answered, a bit annoyed. There should be a law preventing people from giving too much advice during one phone call.

"You should cut your losses, while you still have time. Anyway, are there any other fashion consultants there in London?"

"Not that I know of – why?"

"There must be a reason for that!"

That sealed it. End of conversation. I was exploring uncharted territories and that was the suggestion I got. Don't go there, because nobody before has done what you're trying to do. If that was correct reasoning we wouldn't have discovered America or sent people to the moon, or invented anything at all.

"OK, Mum: I've got to go."

"Sure, take care. Ta-ta."

CHAPTER 19

Ritchie appeared in the office a few days afterward, sheepish and embarrassed. He sat at his desk, but didn't do anything – just sat staring at the computer screen, not typing or browsing the internet, or even playing solitaire. I would have said something, but I was in the middle of trading my stuff and frankly I wasn't in the mood for talking.

He approached me half an hour later.

"GiGi, I know we're in trouble but things are going well with Jonathan, and I'm frightened by what we're going through. I think I need some stability."

"I know, Ritchie. He's a great guy." I answered,

trying not to show my emotions.

"He is. The fact is, I need to be able to count on a regular income, if we want to buy a house and live together. You know me; I wouldn't accept him sustaining me while we're struggling with this business …"

"No need to explain. Do you want to leave?" Tears were just a second away: talk a bit more, GiGi, and you can put the Dambusters to shame. Flooding in south of England; the government suggests you put sandbags around your house and do not exit unless strictly necessary, maybe in a boat.

"I … Yes, I think I need to have something more … permanent. I mean, not that this was not permanent, but …" No need to explain my friend; I know it's been a rollercoaster, with good fun but also scary moments. I can't blame you if you want a regular income.

"Ritchie, it's fine. Come on, don't get emotional; I'll cope."

"I …"

"I had some money put away, I can still pay your salary and your notice," I lied.

"Are you sure? You told me …" – a light of hope was in his eyes, but I had to turn it off before he reconsidered.

"Not to carry on. I'll probably have to give away this fancy office. And if you have to travel back to Berkshire, now that you're settling here, it wouldn't be worth it."

"Oh, GiGi …"

"Here." I handed him a letter with a cheque "It's what is due, plus your share of the bonus."

"GiGi …"

"I can give you a reference anytime you want. Oh, and pick up a list of our vendors, I guess you might want to see if they have a job for you."

"How can I thank you? I feel so guilty leaving you like this." Now he was the one starting to snivel, and if he stayed a bit longer we were going to do our own remake of the Bridges of Madison County.

"Don't. We had a good ride. Find a decent job and if you need a reference, just let me know."

We hugged and sobbed and then he left, leaving me alone in the office, not sure about what I would do next.

My savings were gone, I had a big hole in my finances and not a prospect or a contract; eBay was so slow and this business was progressing like a one-legged man in a kickass contest.

Maybe I should have called in some favours, calling some old customers and … and what? I had already sorted them out. Unless … unless I started a new program, a review, checking out how were they doing (for a small fee) and correcting any mistakes – a sort of sponsor like the ones in the AA, to keep them sober from bad clothing and unmatched garments.

Maybe there was something there. Through the years I'd accumulated a considerable number of names and many of those were not repeat customers. My business was to always count on fresh blood, new people to help: but what about my customer base; all those that had already benefited from my services? They knew me, they knew how I worked. It was worth a try, but not today, I had enough emotion on my plate.

I left the office and started wandering the streets; I don't know how long I walked. I spent most of the time going around Battersea Park, which had been, in the past, a favourite spot for duelling. If I only knew who my enemy was, I could fight, I could find countermeasures in order to protect myself, the people around me and my own business. But something was eluding me; there was something that I knew I hadn't nailed yet. The model was sound, the customers were happy (well, except for one), but money wasn't pouring in. We just got by and we couldn't upscale. I almost forgot that Ritchie was out of the picture, so "I couldn't upscale the business". I wasn't too upset with him; after all, he had to think about his future and this was my own vocation. But not having him around made things even more difficult: no more chats, no more support or a shoulder to cry on.

There were a few people walking around, couples probably in love, mothers with their children and a few bystanders sitting on the grass. I kept walking and soon enough I crossed the bridge in the general direction of Knightsbridge; maybe I should have gone to Harrods and tried to cheer myself up a bit. Instead, I turned right into Eaton Square and continued until I reached Buckingham Palace. It was almost lunchtime and I had a friend working there (No, not That one: an employee) and maybe she'd be free to grab a quick lunch with me.

"Lillian?" I asked when she answered the phone. You never know who's going to answer when you call Buckingham Palace.

"Is it you, GiGi?"

"Yeah, I was in the area and I was wondering if you wanted to grab lunch with me."

It was a long shot and I didn't know if she was even at work, so I kept walking.

"Gimme ten minutes and I'll be outside. Do you remember where?"

I did and I told her. I was already there, so I spent some time doing tourist spotting. The police officer on duty, the tallest man I've ever seen in my life, started getting interested. After all, I wasn't moving like all the others: just standing there, looking suspicious. He probably thought I was trying to sneak in without being noticed. Eventually Lillian came out; she made a gesture as if to say, "It's OK, she's with me" and she kissed me on the cheeks.

"How long has it been, four months?" she asked, while we walked off in the direction of her favourite restaurant. We always went to a little Italian one just two blocks away, which I loved, by the way.

"Yes; last time we met was the dinner at my place, remember? How's Tom?"

"Oh, he's fine. He's still a locum and we're going to move in together next week."

"House-warming party, when?" I asked.

"It's going to be more of a house-painting party. The house is a mess, so we were seriously thinking of inviting people to help with decorating. Are you in? We provide the beers." She laughed, but I knew money was tight and every bit of help would be welcome.

"Why not? Do I have the choice of colours?"

"Yeah, magnolia or magnolia. Just kidding; we haven't decided yet." We reached the restaurant and a young woman showed us our table, which I'd booked while I was still walking towards the palace. Tom and Lillian had been together for almost a year and they were made for each other. He was a young lawyer and a good friend of Helena's. I met the couple a few years back and immediately clicked with Lillian. Since then we had always kept in touch, and when we couldn't meet in person we exchanged messages on Facebook.

"So, how's the business?" she asked, "Still trying to save the world from bad fashion?"

"Sort of, but we got some bad news recently from a client who won't pay."

What are you doing, GiGi? I said to myself. Did you walk all these miles just to complain and talk about your misfortune? You're better than that. Everybody has issues, but that doesn't really mean you have to afflict all your friends with yours. Come on, get a grip: head up, straighten your shoulders and, most of all, don't cry.

"Do you need Tom's help?" she volunteered.

Tom was a great person and surely he would have made a stink if he knew what had happened, but I wasn't looking for revenge or to be paid. It was my decision.

"No, I'm fine. Just a bit sad because Ritchie left." That was a euphemism; actually I was shattered.

"I can't believe that. You two were inseparable." She was really surprised, and so was I. She put the menu down and looked me straight in the eye, waiting for some further comments that I didn't have.

"I know, but we're broke and he needs to think about his future as well. It's understandable, with his new boyfriend and the rest."

"Ritchie is finally settling down? I can't believe it. GiGi, we have to get in touch more often. So what will you do?"

"I've got a couple of ideas that I want to explore." I answered, knowing very well it was a lie. I just had one, and it was untested. Our lunch arrived and for once I ordered a beer with it; an orange juice just wouldn't do.

"Are you seeing someone?" asked Lillian, while attacking her sea-bream and potatoes.

"There's this Jasper guy I'm seeing, but nothing has happened yet. He's a big cheese in fashion, and he offered me a job also." While I was saying it, I realised I'd never thought of what I was going to do next with him. I was attracted to Jasper, but at the same time I had this gut feeling that something wasn't right.

"Are you taking it?"

"Nah, I want my independence. But it caused attrition with Ritchie." I told her the full story, including the fact that Jasper didn't want him and my refusal because of that. She knew already how much I did for the firm and for Ritchie.

"Well, if it doesn't work out, we have a backup: this nice young chef. He was Tom's client in a dispute over a restaurant here in London. We ended up being friends. He'll be at the house-warming party. GiGi, if I wasn't happily married I'd be all over him like a rash. I actually dreamed he was cuddling me last night; he's a sort of Hugh Jackman, just sexier."

"That's hard to believe." She knew I'd always had a crush on Hugh, ever since I first saw him in *Paperback Hero*. I was wondering if she was just teasing me or what.

"You never told me when the house-warming party is."

"Oh, next Friday evening. Dinner, sleeping on the floor and then from Saturday morning it's going to be a painting job. Bring an inflatable mattress. We want to get ready before the furniture starts arriving the following week."

At that point, my phone rang. It was Jasper. I signalled to Lillian that it was him, I excused myself and went outside the restaurant to take the call. He invited me for dinner that very evening; apparently, he'd booked a restaurant – one of the fancy Michelin-starred ones in Mayfair and he wanted me to be there. I said "yes" and we agreed that he'd pick me up at the office. Great! I still had mixed feelings about him and I wasn't sure if going out would actually be a good idea.

We finished lunch with the promise of meeting up during the weekend, after I'd extorted from her the promise of lending me some "painting clothes". I was usually a mess on those sorts of things and no way was I going to ruin mine.

CHAPTER 20

After lunch I had to run home to get changed.

Home.

It wasn't yet home; I'd left my apartment in Berkshire two months previously and was renting one in London, so I could be closer to the office. At that time it had seemed a good idea. After a quick shower it was time to get ready. I put some music on, and started thinking about what to wear for the evening. I didn't want to be too elegant, or let him think I was wearing something too special just for him. After a quick analysis (I didn't need my app) I settled for a pair of Levi's leggings in camo, a pair of high-heeled black shoes, a multi-coloured top by Belle Sauvage and a Lug Von Siga black jacket.

Everything was already listed on eBay and the clock was ticking, but I wanted to wear the outfit one last time before the painful goodbye, which for some items would be the following day. Oh well, never mind, I thought; I'll be able to rebuild my clothing empire one of these days.

I drank some milk from the fridge, directly from the container, and I was ready to go.

Jasper was already at my office, waiting in his car, when I arrived.

"So, tomorrow's the big day," I mentioned, after he'd kissed me on the cheek. "Don't you have things to do, like last-minute checking or something like that?" I remembered when Ritchie and I had opened the office in London, neither of us had been able to sleep for a week, and we spent the night before in the office, checking that everything was in order for our guests the following day. We both crashed on the sofas at three in the morning, just to get up with backache and looking like Zombies.

"I have people taking care of the details," he answered. "That's the advantage of being the Boss. If you worked for me, probably you would be in the shop by now."

We chatted a bit about the opening; he described the layout they had chosen (I made a mental note that he hadn't actually invited me to see the work in progress), and by then we had reached the restaurant.

It was a nice building in Mayfair, not too far

from Oxford Street. The restaurant inside was buzzing with people and the environment was very elegant, although maybe a bit too modern for my taste. We sat by a window and soon a waiter came by asking what we wanted to drink. Jasper chose a bottle of red wine that I'd never heard of, and we both settled for the tasting menu. Big mistake!!

I soon realised that, with ten tasting dishes, there was no room left for actually talking and enjoying the evening. I would start to say something and "bing" – the waiter appeared with the first course. He followed it with a detailed explanation of every single ingredient (apparently, they don't give a name to dishes any more) and how the cook prepared it. I wanted to ask where they were sourcing their products, just for fun, but then thought otherwise. He could have answered.

I had just put a bite in my mouth, when the same guy came back and asked if everything was OK. "Yef, very goof. Fhenk you," I tried to answer, while still chewing. Sometimes I think they do it on purpose, for spite. And the same happened for every single one of the ten courses. Of course, being a very buzzy restaurant, we also got the occasional visit from other waiters passing by, who also decided to ask "Is everything OK?" just to be sure. Politeness prevented us from saying what we really thought!

The dinner was a disaster. Tasty indeed, but, I would have liked to have the chance of saying something to Jasper without being interrupted.

When they finally asked if we wanted a coffee, I took the chance and asked for the bill. Can someone get me out of here?

"Want to come to my place?" asked Jasper when we finally left and reached the car.

"That would be nice. You don't have waiters at your place, right?"

"Ha, ha, ha. No, I promise. They were a bit persistent, weren't they?"

"Persistent? They were like trained pit bulls; they should work as slaves in an S/M shop."

"Yeah, that was a bit excessive. But they were doing their job. Some people like to be pampered, you know?" he said.

"Can you drive?" I asked

"Yeah; maybe you don't remember, but I just had one glass – you supped all the rest."

Dear Jasper, if you'd had had a day like mine, you would sup a bottle as well, I thought. His place was a nice detached property, not too far from where we'd eaten, which made me wonder why we didn't just walk. We entered and I got a sort of déjà vu. Same style as Paula – maybe she had a job as interior decorator. Very similar paintings were on the walls, the furniture all adjusted nicely and with grace. This was not the crash pad of a divorced man; there was too much attention to the detail.

I didn't comment and went straight to the sofa, took my shoes off to get comfy, and couldn't have cared less if he agreed with my doing that or not.

"Want some more wine?" he asked.

"That would be nice; I have actually had a bad day." He went into the kitchen and came back with a couple of glasses in one hand and a bottle of red in the other. He poured the wine and passed me a glass. We clinked glasses, even if in reality I had very little reason to cheer, and I took a sip of mine. It was a Burgundy; that was as far as I could go with wines, and it was tasty and rich. Just like the chap sitting at my side.

"So, what happened today? What made you so grumpy?" he pressed.

"Oh, nothing special. First, I agreed to pay back your ex-wife, and then Ritchie walked out of the door to find a new job. I have half of my stuff on eBay and I don't know what I should do next. Is that enough?" I wasn't grumpy, although I wasn't a happy bunny either. Why should I be?

"I didn't know about Ritchie. You can still come and work for my department store. We could use some of your ideas," he said.

I thought about that for long enough. Ritchie or not, I wanted my independence, the freedom of what I was doing and most of all, to make friends and build a reputation. It was not all about money and selling stuff. The most important thing was to connect with people and make them feel better about themselves. I doubted he could offer me that in his mall.

"With all the buttons you can push, you keep insisting on the same one." I teased him.

"Well, it is a nice one," he said. I moved closer,

sipped a bit more wine and looked at his eyes. They were dark, intense and direct, the sort that make you feel uncomfortable, charmed you – or the kind that make you feel naked, which I preferred much more as an analogy at that point.

He rested his arm on the back of the sofa and his hand was right near my shoulder; his fingers started playing with my hair. Come on, Jasper, I thought: kiss me!

He rested his glass on the little table by the sofa and got closer. No need to spend any more time talking. I had imagined many times where and when we would kiss, and every time it was different in my dreams. I imagined walking among the streets of London with him, hand in hand, when he would suddenly stop and kiss me. Or a classical one: on my doorstep, once he had dropped me home from a long night out (I know, a bit of a cliché, but I can be romantic, you know?).

He got closer; our lips were inches apart and I could feel his breath on me. He was taking his time, letting me savour the moment, while he was relishing the instant he would kiss me, finally.

It was sudden and passionate, and although I didn't know Jasper well I was attracted to him. Tonight I didn't want to be alone; I wanted to end the day on a positive note, after all the negative ones.

I climbed on Jasper and started kissing him, on his lips and on his neck, while at the same time removing his tie and unbuttoning his shirt.

We made love right there on the sofa, and then again in his bed, until we both lay there exhausted. Sleep caught us suddenly, while we still were in each other's arms.

CHAPTER 21

I woke up in the morning and the sun was starting to filter through the curtains, on a rare sunny day. With my arm I started searching for Jasper, but he wasn't there. Today was the opening, so probably he had left … hang on: I could hear noise from the kitchen and a nice smell of bacon. It was seven in the morning.

I grabbed a dressing gown from the en suite and followed the smell like a greyhound on a track until I found the kitchen. Jasper was fully dressed, chewing the last remnants of his bacon sandwich while standing by the sink and ready to go. I could see his black briefcase on the table.

"I've got to go, honey. I've got a department

store to open."

Honey?

He gave me a kiss on the cheek and added: "Do what you want; have some breakfast. You can leave the keys with reception; talk to you later." And off he went.

Honey?

What the frock? I wasn't expecting to be served breakfast in bed, but honey, stopping for a hug wouldn't have jeopardised your grand opening. By the way, if this was my place I would have bothered to prepare breakfast for him (and not just myself) and make an effort to be nice, even if I had to open Buckingham Palace that very same morning.

What is wrong with men? Do they forget things? Being nice is free, you know! Really, it doesn't cost a thing. Had I made a mistake?

Something was out of place, and I still couldn't put my finger on what it was. Even his apartment didn't look right. The more I looked at it, the more I could smell the scent of Paula, her touch, her style. But they were divorced; I knew that for a fact, and even Harry had confirmed it when we were there. Can you still divorce a person and then have her sorting out your furniture? Is that legally allowed? Or maybe they had the apartment before they split and he hadn't changed anything. Well, that sounded a more plausible explanation, although I couldn't live in a place that an ex-partner had furnished. Too many memories that would be under my nose on a daily basis; I would scream for a change.

I let the thought of all that slip away and went to have a shower. I had work to do as well and possibly Jasper was just nervous about the opening.

Back at the office I felt as sad as ever, while I prepared a cup of tea for me and nobody else. The joy I had shared with Ritchie was gone, sucked out of the place, now empty and silent. I peeked out of the window and I could see people queuing up at the Battersea Fashion Centre. I couldn't believe how many people were standing there, even more than if One Direction themselves were throwing a free-for-all party and had announced it on Facebook.

I sipped my tea and went back to the computer. The general idea was to contact all the previous customers I'd had and offer an "assessment": a re-evaluation of their wardrobe, see if everything was still current and, most of all, if they were sticking to the plan. As I had many of them, I thought I wouldn't spam them all at once. I didn't know how many responses I would get, and I wasn't going to disappoint them by saying I wouldn't have time to see them until two weeks later. Ten at a time would be enough. Preparing the messages took a couple of hours, but finally I was ready to send them out. I made ten different versions, personalised and specific to each client. In no way, shape or form was I going to deal with them as if they were only "clients"; we had shared so many things, emotions and personal stories that they were far more than that. We'd had an experience together that deserved to be remembered and renewed, not an impersonal customer service like anybody else could think of or do.

I pressed the "send" button and felt relieved, as if I were still in business. The next step was to arrange some small advertisements. A quick check on eBay brought a bit of light to what otherwise would have been a grim day. People were bidding fast, especially on the samples and the items that never met the shops – those unique clothes and items that you could be sure nobody else was going to wear to a party. I would possibly have to spend the evening packing and preparing labels.

I had another peek out of the window and the queue was gone; maybe all the people were inside already. How much would they make in a single day?

After I'd spent another hour playing solitaire at the computer, I was ready to pack up and go home when "ding" – I got an email.

It was from Natalie, a brunette in her thirties from Ascot with whom I had worked a couple of years ago.

Dear GiGi

How lovely hearing from you! I was just thinking

about you the other day, and, looking at my current outfit, I thought I was in need of a, how should I say, "refreshment".

Please don't get me wrong, I still enjoy many of the clothes you suggested and most of all I treasure all your precious suggestions.

Do you remember all the laughs we had telling each other stories?

Unfortunately, I'm undergoing a divorce. After many years of marriage, my husband decided he needed a brand new Porsche and to pair that with a bimbo. They say it's something occasionally people do when they reach their forties. Please don't be sad for me; the lawyer says I'm going to have a fantastic settlement. In addition, I have had so many men hovering around me over the past two years that my ex-husband's disappearance will go unnoticed. So my thoughts went to you and, what I hoped, a brand-new wardrobe. You see, great minds think alike! It might be some astral conjunction that brought us together today. If you're happy about it, I would also like to propose another job. Maybe a bit unusual, but I trust your judgement and ethics to tell me if I'm way out of line.

Would it be too much trouble to come around today or tomorrow? I know it's very short notice and if that's inconvenient, please let me know.

Looking forward to hearing from you,
Your dear friend and forever-grateful Natalie

That was unexpected. I had sent those emails

half-heartedly, trying to keep myself busy and keep my hopes up. Maybe I wasn't going to go bankrupt just yet. I didn't hesitate.

Dear Natalie.

Sorry to hear about the news. No problem whatsoever to come round today. Imagine I'm already in my car heading for your place. If I see the bastard on the road, I shall run him over. See you soon

Kisses,
GiGi

I grabbed my bag, car keys and a few ideas and in no time I was out of the door, driving towards Berkshire. I tried to remember every single detail about Natalie and what she'd bought, but I realised when I arrived that a new job was facing me. She had shed at least three stone and now she looked like a bundle of muscles. Or like an iron-man champion. Anyway, I saw clearly why she needed some help; everything had been built around hiding her weight and for sure, what she had would look very baggy and horrible now. The good news was that she was a "healthy stick", not the type to have lost weight owing to a tragedy.

"You look fabulous!" I said, as soon as she opened the door. "How did you do that?"

"Oh, it wasn't that hard, dear. The bastard decided to have his middle-age crisis and I decided to join the local gym. But don't stand there: come in." She gave me a hug and a kiss on the cheek and we went inside.

"Shall I put the kettle on?"

"That would be very nice, Natalie," I answered promptly.

"Can you imagine? A wardrobe full of things that now I can't wear, and I had to resort to onesies – at my age!"

"With that figure you can wear what you want," I lied. I wasn't a fan of onesies, especially of those in an animal shape, with ears, tail and the whole shebang. Apparently, she wasn't the only one in need of a revamp; the house looked a bit old as well. I looked around and sat on an old leather sofa that had seen better times. Not bad, but a bit dated as a style. I made a mental note to bring the matter up.

"So, Natalie," I shouted from the lounge, "what kind of exercise are you doing in the gym?"

"Oh, I'm not missing anything these days. I started with the usual weightlifting, and then I got introduced to aerobics. Then I discovered Zumba and I thought, *why not?* So I gave it a try."

"Wow. You keep yourself busy."

She came back with a pot of tea, cups and a few biscuits. "I can now afford to eat those little fellas without feeling guilty. I also started spinning and bodystep." She grabbed a chocolate one and devoured it before I could say "treadmill". She was really in great shape and what baffled me was why in hell her husband would look somewhere else. So I asked.

"I got over it. The love was gone years ago, and we were just tolerating each other. The bimbo was inevitable, and in some respects I'm glad of it. It saved me the hassle of dumping him."

"Got it. So I guess now you'll need to find some Wonder Woman garments?" I laughed, nervously at the beginning, but she followed suit so I relaxed. I was glad that all those hours spent in the gym hadn't changed her.

"Well, I'd be glad of a style that would make the most of my new body; and I need some help spending my settlement. Can you assist me in fulfilling my current buy-sexual desire?"

I'd never heard of that, so I started giggling. "So, what's your budget?" I asked.

"I guess forty grand on clothes, I already have more jewellery than I could ever need or want." An idea started forming in my mind; although I wasn't sure how to articulate it.

"Natalie, let me get this straight. You're in great shape. You're also going to have a great look, so men will start queuing up to take you out and eventually you'll invite someone home. You know the drill: will you come in for a drink, watch a bit of telly, spend some quality time talking …"

I could see her head spinning. She hadn't even considered how old-fashioned her place was, and what's the point of being the hottest chick at the gym if then you have to take a date into Dracula's den?

"I see your point. The place looks outdated, right?" she said, starting to look around her, as if the furniture had suddenly just appeared in front of her.

"You told me you got some of these pieces from your family and others were bought with Thomas. Why don't you pick just the things you really like, and then get some new furniture that would fit better with the new you?"

"Sounds like you have a new job on your hands. What do you know about furniture?" she asked, looking deeply into my eyes.

"Not much, Natalie; it's not my forte. It was just a suggestion, something to think about," I added sheepishly. It wasn't my intention to present myself as an interior designer; I was just concerned that there would be an imbalance between the new look and where she lived. "Maybe if you like the idea I could come along, as a friend. It could be an art I might want to learn."

"Deal. I'm sure you'll do more than tag along, so we need to think about a fee for this extra help. What about getting rid of all my oversized clothes? I'm sure you'll find ways."

That was tempting. In addition to my fee, I would take home a huge amount of items that I could flog on the underground market. And believe me, in those places, size sixteen and eighteen were always sold at a premium, as they were very difficult to come by.

"I'm very glad about that. I was thinking: would it be too much trouble to have half the fee when we've done half of the job?"

"Not a problem, GiGi. But I didn't ask: is everything OK with you? You aren't as cheerful as I remember." I told her about the latest mishap with Lady Whilsham, and how Jasper's reaction bothered me in the morning.

"If you feel it's wrong, it probably is. Trust me; I had ignored any possible signals, thinking I was just deluded and jealous. Life is too short to try fixing things, my dear. If a relationship is too much of an effort, it isn't worth it."

We started that very day, planning the new look. She was going to be great again in no time. I wasn't so sure about me though.

CHAPTER 22

The day was gone (pretty much) so I didn't bother returning to the office, and instead I went straight home for a shower. I was glad I had re-established a relationship with Natalie and the new task of sorting out her home excited me. Challenging. Thrilling. Electrifying.

I had a brief look at my email account and saw that I'd received an email from another customer asking for a review, so I was thrilled. I thought of calling Ritchie, but I froze; I wasn't in a position yet to offer him a job. I thought of calling Jasper and, at that very moment, I realised how upset I was feeling towards him, and I needed to chill. I opened a bottle of Shiraz and slept the whole night on the sofa.

The following day I had the right idea about Natalie; she had a great body and so we should use a Hervé Léger style, all centred around bodycons and very tight clothes. She was like a statue, so she might as well show it to the world. I had to banish all those clothes in which you could barely distinguish her figure; a new Natalie was going to be born this week.

What confused me slightly was the furniture task. I mean, I was no interior designer and maybe I should have called my old friend. I dialled the number and got an answering machine. I decided not to leave a message. I then thought that I should have approached the matter in the same way as with clothes; look at the personality, GiGi, and see if and how things fit and belong. So off I went scouting and in search of new ideas.

I finished my quest earlier because that very evening Lillian had the house-warming party. I stopped at the local newsagent, bought all the possible magazines about interior design, and placed them on my desk. There would have to be some catching up to do in the next few days, but now my attention was on the up-and-coming party.

Don't you hate it when you know you have to dress casual (possibly trashy) and at the same time you know the most gorgeous man is going to be present? There's no rule for that type of situation. Go dressed like a sack of potatoes and he'll never notice you. Go and dress half-decently, and in his eyes you'll look like a pretentious bitch who couldn't be bothered to get changed and help a friend with a little painting. I only hoped Lillian wasn't exaggerating when she said he looked like Hugh Jackman. At that point the phone rang, and it was Jasper.

"Hi Jasper; what do you want?" I asked abruptly. Maybe he could hear from my voice he still needed to apologise.

"I called to offer you a job in my store."

"Aren't you tired of that line, Jasper? You keep repeating yourself over and over."

"That's because you're the best and I need you in my shop; to make it unique," he insisted, but I wasn't in the mood for jokes.

"This might come as a surprise, but the answer is still 'no'. Get over it."

"OK, message received." He sounded disappointed and harsh for a moment and I was ready to fight. Come off it, Jasper: you have to learn when it's time to let it go and move on. "What about coming to visit the department store at least? You haven't shown up yet."

I would have gone, actually, if he could have been bothered to invite me. That was something he had forgotten; he'd never actually asked me to come over and have a look at how the work was proceeding, or even to summon me to the big opening. The only thing he could say was to repeat 'Come and work for me,' like a broken record. "And after the visit maybe we could go out for dinner."

I'd made that mistake once; I would have been stupid to do it twice. Just to not sound too abrupt, I chose delicacy over iron fist. "I'd like to see that little shop of yours, if you don't mind, but for this evening I have previous arrangements."

"Can I come along? Anybody I know?"

"No, Jasper." He was like a bloody pit bull; he wouldn't let it go. "It's a girlie night," I said to cut him short.

"OK, GiGi. See you when you come here. Ask at reception and I shall come and get you for the tour."

I thought of skipping even that invite, but then I thought, what the hell? – it's just a shop, although humongous. Let's have a peek and see what it's all about.

I had a quick shower and then drove down to the Battersea Fashion Centre. Once inside I reached a huge information desk, which was in the middle of the ground floor. People were buzzing around it; there were free-standing touch screens where people could find information and some large displays with the layout of the shop and where to find things. I approached one of the girls at the reception and gave her my name, said I was looking for Jasper Barnes. She nodded and punched numbers into a phone, and after a quick exchange, she informed me Jasper would arrive soon. I looked around me and didn't get what all the fuss was about. The ground floor was exactly the same as you could find in any other department store, mostly dedicated to perfumes and make-up. If they did something special, it passed unnoticed by me. Jasper arrived after a few minutes, gliding among employees, providing a smile now on the left, now on the right, stopping for a second just to sort out a minuscule detail he alone could see.

He reached for me. "GiGi, how beautiful you are today. So what do you think; it's impressive, isn't it?"

Don't you HATE it when people ask questions and give themselves the answer? I mean, what use do they have for other people? They're perfect by themselves, asking the perfect questions all the time and never getting tired of listening to their own answers. I wondered if Jasper ever disagreed with himself. The ground floor was as expected: the very same as many other places and department stores you could find on a high street, but the first floor was slightly more interesting. Different fashion labels were occupying this level, each one having a fifteen-by-twenty-foot area to expose. It was an impressive area – maybe the largest display of clothes you could find is a single space – but I couldn't stop thinking that maybe, just maybe, Jasper had lost his one chance to do something original. The more we wandered around, the more the feeling that he'd got it wrong became more persistent. Nothing that anybody else would notice – on the contrary, the shop was very nice; but it wasn't innovative. The only impressive thing was the sheer size of that building and that was, in my opinion, the biggest mistake he'd made so far. By going humongous, he thought of serving every human in this world; in his shop everybody would be able to find whatever they needed, and that was a fundamental mistake. The quality of the designer labels he had there was high, and that meant he couldn't really discount too much. These were not warehouse remnants, samples, last year's designs: these were current-season fashion. I knew where he was going: pile them up and sell them (fairly) cheaply, which in this case was only a fifteen or twenty per cent discount. Reduce his margins and try to squeeze the competition out of the game, as they wouldn't be able to afford the same reductions in the long run.

But, as I said, there was a flaw: recurring customers.

The underground warehouses where I used to go were working on a different principle, that of uniqueness. And a shortage of items. There's nothing better, both for a shop and to attract a woman, than to hold unique items – something that won't be easily available to other people. We need to think that the skirt we're buying won't be seen anywhere else in the world. In addition, the underground warehouses were also playing on the scarcity of items, enticing people to come back at regular intervals to see what new items and pieces were available. Failing to find what we were looking for (assuming we knew in the first place), we'd make a compulsive purchase based purely on frustration.

All of this aspect was missing in Jasper's monstrous shop: the shopping experience.

I was mulling over all those considerations when I heard a familiar voice shouting, not far from where we were standing. I looked in the general direction and there she was, Lady Whilsham, shouting her head off at some poor shop assistant.

"YOU ARE AN IDIOT! CAN'T YOU SEE WHAT YOU'VE JUST DONE? ALL THIS AREA NEEDS TO BE REDONE!"

I was surprised, not only to find her here in the shop, but also to see her acting as if she owned the place.

"PACK YOUR THINGS AND LEAVE NOW! YOU'RE FIRED!"

Indeed, Paula was doing her best impression of Sir Alan Sugar, including pointing the index finger at the poor girl while she was giving her the sack. I looked at Jasper as if to ask for an explanation. What he had to say I didn't like one bit.

"She's my partner in this endeavour. She put up half of the capital."

"Can't you do something???" I asked. I couldn't see anything wrong with the stand the girl was working at, except maybe it was a tad dull; but hey, the whole Battersea Fashion Centre was dull.

"Not really. As I said, she owns half of this place." He was very relaxed and couldn't have cared less about what was happening under his very eyes. Paula saw me arguing with Jasper, and a victory grin suddenly appeared on her face.

"Come on, Jasper, you can do better than giving me the 'business is business' crap. You know there's nothing wrong with that stall."

"GiGi, maybe you shouldn't get involved in these matters, especially as you've decided not to be part of all this."

W-H-A-T????

What kind of bloody corporate monster had I got involved with? Sure, if I was working here, I could have easily told off Lady HalfCapital and voiced my concerns about the way she was handling the employees. Oh, come off it!

"Maybe I shouldn't get involved in anything you're doing," I snapped back.

"GiGi, I don't think …"

"If I'd accepted your offer, is this what I could have expected? To be spoken to as if I were a schoolgirl?"

"Excuse me," Lady Whilsham interjected "I don't think you have the right …"

"No, I do not have any right, but either you've made a mistake now in firing that girl, or you made a mistake in hiring her in the first place. And I bet you don't have any idea what I'm talking about."

"I don't think …" she tried to say again.

"Yeah: that's the problem. Jasper, see you around. I've just remembered I have more important things to do." And so I stormed off out of the shop, leaving poor Jasper scratching his head and thinking what the hell was wrong with me. I couldn't have cared less.

I went back to my car and gave a quick glance at my darkened office window and sighed. I had a party to attend that night.

CHAPTER 23

Lillian and Tom's house was a semi-detached near Amersham, and for once I arrived on time (usually I'm early). Eventually I'd decided to take a day off from fashion and, instead of the outfit I'd decided on earlier, I settled for an easy pair of jeans and a shirt – something I could cover in paint and not shed a single tear over. Plus another pair as a change, as ugly and used as the first one, stored in a canvas bag I'd found at the bottom of my car boot.

When I rang the bell, Tom came to open the door, "Excuse me: may I help you?"

I smiled and said, "Of course. I'm from the council and I want to ensure you adhere to our policy about painting your interior. In particular, blue and green should never be seen."

"Oh my gosh, GiGi, I didn't expect you. I mean, I did expect you, but not dressed like that. What happened to you; did you lose the lottery?" We laughed at my attire which, I must admit, was very uncharacteristically grungy. Then I took a good look at Tom and considered that he must have borrowed his clothing from an interior decorator. It was ill-fitting and covered from head to toe in paint, despite that part of the party not even having started yet. (I praised myself, as I'd even put my hair up and had a scarf to hand to save my well-coiffured locks from getting covered in paint – I'd been organised, for once!) I couldn't resist, though; I had to know whose clothes Tom had borrowed, so I asked. He gave such a belly laugh that I knew there had to be a good story behind that one, though he didn't seem to be inclined to spill the beans. See, the thing is, you'd have to picture Tom. He was already on the chubby side, and that's putting it kindly, so to have borrowed someone else's clothes, and for those clothes to almost drown him, they'd have to have been pretty big. Don't get me wrong, Tom was by no means short; Lillian would never make do with a shortie with a chip on his shoulder. Lillian heard Tom's laughter and came to investigate. She ran up to me, gave me a great big hug and kisses on both cheeks. Yes, I know, that's very Continental, but that's how we are with each other. (Someone on the street in

Britain might just think that we were lovers, the way we greet each other sometimes.) Her words came gushing out in her excitement, and not quite as quietly as she would have liked either, that the "Hugh Jackman look-alike" was already there and enjoying a beer in the kitchen, discussing recipes with Julian and his new girlfriend. This was the first time that Tom and Lillian had met her and so, as per the norm, Lillian had already forgotten her name. It was going to have to be left to Tom to introduce her. I started to follow Lillian to the kitchen, to deposit my prerequisite bottles, but just then the doorbell rang. Lillian turned to look to see who it might be, with her fingers crossed.

"Why are you crossing your fingers?" I asked.

"I'm hoping that Ritchie decided to accept our invitation, despite the bad blood between the two of you currently," came her reply.

"How could you invite him? I haven't been able to reach him in days; he definitely won't want to come along, because he's still mad at me. Can you believe, he won't even pick up the phone? All I want to do is mend the broken bridges between us, especially now that I may be almost back on track and I shall shortly, hopefully, be able to give him his job back."

Lillian then let out a long sigh whilst Tom attended to the door. I turned to look at what had caused her to do that, as she was no longer looking in the direction of the front door, but the kitchen. As soon as I set eyes on him, I knew the reason for the sigh. He was Gorgeous, with a capital G. "Oh, my god," I whispered to Lillian. "You weren't exaggerating when you described him as 'Hugh Jackman'." I could clearly see that even Lillian's tongue was almost hanging out. He had dark hair and was tall, with a slightly Mediterranean complexion. And he was gorgeous. Really gorgeous. Did I mention that he was gorgeous?

"Raffaele, this is GiGi, the friend I talked to you about."

"Call me Raf. Hello: Lillian speaks very highly of you, or better, now that I think about it, she's always speaking about you."

"Probably only gossip, given her line of work," I said. Lillian gave me a light punch on the shoulder.

"Hey, don't be rude, or tomorrow you'll have the small paintbrush. I'll give you the job of doing all the fiddly bits," she teased me.

"What did she say? I'm very curious," I urged him.

"Mostly about your line of work, which strikes me as very atypical. You might see all sorts of people."

"Indeed; however, most of my customers then become friends. How did you meet Lillian?"

"Actually, I'm a friend of Tom's. He helped me with some issues I had with the restaurant I was working for. Now I'm just about to open my own."

"Oh, you're a cook …" I teased him.

"I prefer saying that I'm a chef, but yes, cooking is what I do for a living."

"A good one?"

"My food hasn't killed anybody yet, so I guess I'm a decent one."

"And then you'd have Tom to keep you out of jail." I couldn't control my mouth, I didn't know if I was trying to be funny or just making conversation, but most of the time I was babbling, while I kept scrutinising the beauty I had in front of me. He had deep, dark eyes that seemed to read my most intimate secrets when he looked at me. I hoped he could not actually do that, or it would have been extremely embarrassing. "Sorry, I didn't mean it like that; I was just kidding. I'm sure you're an excellent cook … erm … chef."

Lillian interjected "He is indeed. Excuse me, but I have other guests to attend to. Don't do anything I wouldn't do while I'm away."

We looked at each other, half embarrassed, or at least I was. Don't let me spill the beans, but I'm sure I would have done something Lillian, being married, would have avoided.

"I notice an accent. Where are you from?"

"Oh, I'm from New York."

"The name sounds Italian, though," I stated.

"You're quite correct; despite my lack of an Italian accent, my father is Italian and my mother American."

"What kind of cooking, pardon, cheffing, are you doing?"

"Ha, ha, ha! I have classical training, but now I'm doing my own thing."

"So, what does it take to get a date with you and be invited for dinner?" I asked cheekily.

"I suppose you have to avoid criticising my food. How badly should I dress, in order to get some free suggestions from you?" he answered back.

"Hmm, let me think. What you're wearing now already qualifies." We both laughed. Despite being in a large shirt and baggy jeans, I'd swear that dressed in that attire he could make the cover of Vogue, in my opinion. That was how blinded I was by him. Can someone compromise just like that on style? Did it take just one beautiful, statuesque, stunning man to change my entire philosophy? This was a matter that needed investigating, and I promised myself not to let the subject go until I was satisfied.

They called us one minute later, while we were still flirting, and for once I cursed the homeowners for that. I did my very best to sit near Raffaele, sneaking behind him and pushing anybody else out of my way (gently but firmly), until I managed to sit on his side of the table.

And so the game of cat and mouse had begun.

Lillian hadn't "volunteered" Raffaele to cook dinner that evening, so I was left with curiosity about his restaurant. "Where is it actually located" I asked. "I mean, the place where you work."

"Oh, it's down in Surrey. I had a decent settlement, thanks to Tom, and decided to open my own place. The restaurant is a bit of a wreck at the moment; it was an attempt to be a gastro pub, many years ago, but the owner made a silly mistake."

"Which was?"

"Well, the pub is bang in this old village, and has been there for many years, but the guy who took over went the Michelin route: you know – silly prices, nouvelle cuisine, removed everything that was local and replaced the beer with expensive wine. His idea was to attract the stockbrokers living in the area, but the only result was that he alienated the villagers."

"How come it's a wreck now?" I asked. From his description it seemed he had a very fancy place; I didn't understand.

"The owner was a rich guy who went back to Australia and set the prices too high for anybody to be interested. That was almost ten years ago. Then he just forgot the place until he died. Youngsters used to break in for fun, or to have a quiet place to get drunk or smoke a joint. It's a graffiti paradise now. The old owner died not long ago and the heirs decided they didn't want any assets in Good Ole England. Then I showed up with my pile of money and they knew I was going to solve their problem."

"So, it actually is a wreck. What about having a restaurant-warming party? Same people as here, who could give you a hand in sorting out the place."

"Could be an idea and would save some bucks,"

he said thoughtfully.

"You'd have to cook, though, or the idea won't fly."

Lillian was ready with the starter, which came from a local deli. They'd had so much to do with the relocation and their busy schedule that asking them to cook as well would have been unfair. The first round of beers came and went and we were preparing for another round. Soon we'd be attacking the food and washing it down with some good wine.

"So, are you seeing someone?" he asked, unexpectedly.

That was a question I still had to ask (and answer) myself. Was I seeing Jasper? That was something I thought I wasn't prepared to deal with, not that evening anyway. Nonetheless, life occasionally forces you to take decisions. Don't get me wrong: I could have answered by saying anything, even told him a lie, but that isn't a good way to start with people, is it? I could have stalled, or possibly I could even have answered with a "none of your business" type of statement (although a politer one) – but the fact was that I wanted it to be his business. No, I was over with Jasper; deep inside I knew we weren't a good fit. Too much of a slippery guy: one second affectionate, the other the worst bastard on earth. And still I couldn't figure out his connection with his ex-wife; what was happening there? Maybe they weren't over yet; maybe there was something else. I hoped I had learned to trust my instinct and I could honestly say that I was through with Jasper.

And then, he'd asked that sort of question for a reason, not just because he was curious.

"Not at the moment," I finally answered, after what seemed like an eternity. I didn't want to ask him the same question; he was obviously free, as Lillian wouldn't be trying to match-make if that wasn't the case. But the recent story with Jasper had dented my confidence. I went quiet for a second and, before our silence became embarrassing, I asked "What kind of food do you cook?"

"As I said, I'm classically trained. I spent some years in France and Italy, but I recently travelled to Thailand and I sort of discovered that kind of cuisine. I haven't tried it yet in a restaurant, though."

"Your restaurant? Will it be a Thai one?"

"No, I have my own style, but it's based on French; maybe in the future I might switch to something more exotic – I don't know yet. I guess it'll evolve. Lillian told me you work in fashion, helping people to find their own style."

And off I went, explaining what I actually did. A couple of other people joined the conversation, which flowed at the same pace as the beers and, later, the wine. I already felt a bit tipsy, but talking with Raffaele was effortless, and after the past week I needed some relaxation and to unwind from all the frustration I'd experienced. A glass or two

BLUE AND GREEN SHOULD NEVER BE SEEN!

helped.

CHAPTER 24

I woke up and my mouth felt like the bottom of a budgie's cage. And I had the mother of all headaches. That's what happens when you go to a painting party; we started, at some point, just drinking some beers and then, not to disappoint the other guests, we also went into full swing tasting each other's wine. Mine was a Custoza sourced from my Italian neighbours directly from a vineyard near Mantua that belonged to their parents.

Oh dear, I also had jelly legs, as if I'd run a marathon, and I was still in my clothes. I looked around and nobody was there; of course, it was almost ten in the morning and I was sure the others were already painting. They might have finished the house by now. What a shame. I crawled to the bathroom and had a cold shower, and when I say cold I mean cold: pieces of ice were falling from the shower rose.

I felt a bit better but not much. Worst of all, I started having flashbacks from the previous evening. Sheepishly, I went downstairs and into the kitchen where, fortunately, other people were still assembled, finishing their breakfast.

"GOOD MORNING, SLEEPY HEAD!" said Lillian, with a voice that sounded to me like thunder and, for a moment, I thought she'd swallowed a megaphone (I doubt that anyone reading this has never felt the same way, at least once in their life).

"G'morning," I heard my mouth saying. "Coffee?"

"UP THERE: THERE'S A FRESH BATCH."

"Could you please stop shouting? I think the aliens took me and implanted bionic ears. I could hear a fly breathing."

"Sure, although rumour has it you can get the same effect after a bottle of Tequila. I never tried, but you should know."

In the meantime, other people came around to say hello, including gorgeous Raffaele.

"Hey, GiGi, we've prepared your declaration of independence," said Tom, showing me a piece of wallpaper with the back finely written on.

"The … what …?"

"The declaration of independence from ugly clothes. You mentioned it yesterday evening, so we thought of capturing your fine words, and then they won't be lost to the planet."

I started remembering. At some point I had an image in my mind of myself, standing on the lounge table and talking about how I would save the world from bad clothing, and the right of the individual to enhance their looks. Plus some other items that, at that point, were still quite foggy.

"We also have a video, but we decided not to post it on YouTube yet. We thought the declaration would make things more formal if it were in writing. Here: it's signed by everybody." Tom handed me my own version of the Magna Carta, I could see the signatures of all the guests at the bottom. Someone had also taken the time to depict a coat of armour, a shield; on one side there was a woman in a coat (?!) brandishing a lipstick, on the other side there were some accessories arranged as a sort of bear-like animal. I was speechless; the guys had taken their time to do the job and had done it really rather well.

"Don't worry; you were funny last night," whispered Raffaele in my ear. I could smell his aftershave and hopefully, from his side, he couldn't smell the tequila that was still permeating from my pores.

"Yeah," interjected Marion, "especially when you cited the Fourth Amendment, when you declared that Raffaele here was dispensed from wearing any clothes, even in winter."

"What was that piece?" asked Lillian "Oh, yes. That was the statement about perfection, the only allowed exception to Her Majesty's ruling."

"Was that before or after she tried to snog him?" continued Marion.

Oh-my-God. I started remembering bits and pieces and my face started to assume every single shade of red from the shame I felt.

"Did I really …?"

"Yes," commented Tom, "there was actually a debate as to whether or not we should let you carry on in your pursuit to see what would happen next. The moderate wing of the parliament decided to stop you," he said, pointing in the general direction of the other girls.

I was grateful for my female friends and their sensitivity in not posting me on YouTube. I would have done it. Whispers could be heard every time I was near Raffaele, but what could I honestly do? I liked the guy. I decided it was time to get some food and decided to fry a couple of eggs and bacon, hoping they would forget about me. That didn't happen. Even as I was in the kitchen with my back to them, trying my best to ignore them, I could still hear them going on and on. Raffaele, on the other hand, seemed quite amused, rather than embarrassed by the situation; but then I realised he'd been on the receiving end of my attentions. Oh my gosh: how could I look him in the eye and make him forget? That scene, which I barely remember, would be between us every time we met.

But in some ways I was also happy it had happened like that; no more circling around, letting him guess that I fancied him and so on. The cat was out of the bag and if he had an interest, it wouldn't take him long to show it. Once breakfast was over, we started working and by chance (or by plot) I found myself painting in the same room as Raffaele.

"That was something," he said. "I mean the speech. You're passionate about your job."

"I suppose so. I just wanted to let you know that usually I don't drink. I mean, a glass once in a while, but I don't remember the last time I trashed myself like that."

"Not to worry; you were entertaining," he said, while attacking a wall with his brush, giving long and resolute strokes of paint. "At the beginning I thought you were full of yourself – all job-oriented, if I may say. In reality, I just think you like what you're doing. We're similar, in some respects."

"In some ways I'm glad it happened; I don't open up easily – like this bloody tin of paint!" I said. I found a screwdriver and I was struggling with it, trying to get the lid off the damn thing, and I almost cut my finger during the first attempt. Raffaele laid his brush on a piece of paper and came around to help me.

"Here, let me do it," he said, taking the screwdriver out of my hands and opening the tin on my behalf. He had strong hands and soft skin, which I felt when he touched me. I wondered how I would have felt in his arms, but very quickly staved off that thought for fear he would read it straight from my eyes. He was also looking at me, and for a moment our eyes locked, perhaps for one second too long. We went back to our work.

Between one stroke of the paintbrush and the next we had time for a few cups of coffee (or tea, in his case) and to get to know each other better; we also had Lillian checking on us from time to time, bringing snacks and munchies which, at that point in mid-morning, were welcome. It was easy to talk to Raffaele; everything flowed and, for once, I felt I could open up to him. I could be my full self, without the fear of being judged or branded "a bit nutty" for what I was trying to do. He could understand that people might have a vision, a desire, and the will to make an effort to live their lives to the full. He was trying to do the same with his own restaurant. We shared some sandwiches and the room was done, far sooner than I would have liked or expected. I would have volunteered to do the rest of the house if Raffaele was going to help me, but eventually all the others also assembled in the lounge and it was time to go.

Lillian and Tom were grateful for our help and we promised each other to get in touch soon. It was time to leave. Fortunately, Raffaele thought of asking for my phone number; I had been on the verge of doing the same, but after what I had done the previous night I wasn't really keen to openly state that I liked him – a lot.

We promised each other that we'd see each other again and would have dinner out. Leaving Lillian's house was a struggle: much more painful that I could have imagined. It was time to go.

CHAPTER 25

My job with Natalie was proceeding well; she loved the new style and the few things we'd bought together had already left their mark. People in the gym were queuing to get her phone number; she'd revamped her Facebook page and people who'd been lost for years suddenly got in touch again. As she was enjoying her new life we thought of celebrating the occasion and immortalising the moment. I gave a call to a photographer friend of mine and, pronto, we were in her gym, ready to do some shooting. We had a set of pictures of her doing exercises and others a bit more sensual, both in colour and black-and-white; then we moved back to her house for more shots, in the garden with some new clothes. Gavin, the photographer, also insisted on some black-and-whites inside the house, just to capture her with the right atmosphere, but we soon realised that everything was out of place. We actually struggled to find the "real" her among all that old-style furniture. She gave me a look as if to say "You told me so," and it didn't take me long to figure out that I would have to tackle the interior of the house as well.

The photos were soon downloaded onto her laptop and went on Facebook straight away, causing uproar among her friends. Natalie was almost in tears reading the responses and she couldn't thank me enough, despite being still in the middle of her make-over.

I had to crack on as well with the furnishing bit and that occasion happened that afternoon at my office. On my workplace doorstep was that girl who had been fired by Lady Whilsham in the Battersea Fashion Centre, sitting in the entranceway and reading a book. She jumped to her feet as soon as she saw me.

"I remember you," I said, while she rearranged her clothes in an attempt to look good.

"My name's Erika, and yes, I saw you in the mall. I was wondering if I could work with you."

"I'm not hiring at the moment; times are tight," I answered while I was opening the door. "Would you like a tea or coffee?" She nodded and followed me inside.

She was in her thirties, brunette and well

dressed. From the way she spoke and presented herself I could see she'd had a good education and also … I couldn't pinpoint it, but there was a sense of self-assurance, determination, that I hadn't spotted when she was in that mall. If I had to bet my last pair of shoes I would have said she was a lawyer. How do you recognise a lawyer from just a look, I asked myself? The more I tried to remove that thought from my mind, the more it came back to haunt me. I even thought of asking, but if she really was one, then in her thirties she wouldn't be working as a shop assistant, would she? I decided to suspend judgement until I had further information about this Erika.

"It doesn't matter if you don't pay me; I just want to learn from you."

"And why should I agree to that?"

"They're worried, over in the mall. They've done things on a very large scale, but it's all so impersonal. I heard Mr. Barnes saying that they don't have an edge on other shops. He's afraid he's going to be branded as a sort of pound shop. And they don't recognise initiative; that's why they fired me." She was talking fast, trying to avoid the awkward question.

"Do you know what I do here?"

"Yes, you're a fashion consultant. You look at individuals and help them to find their own style." Well, that was it in a nutshell: I couldn't have said it better myself.

"OK, here's what we're going to do." I picked

up a folder from a random client of mine, removed the personal details and left only the clothes pictures. "Here's two hundred pounds. Look at this file, buy some interior-design magazines, the more the merrier, and come back with ideas on how you would style this person's house. You've got two days."

"I don't understand." She looked at me, baffled, first looking at the money I had given her, then at me, and then back to the money. "You want me to do interior design … I thought … Who's the owner; what would they like …?"

"Erika, you said you're smart and have initiative. Figure it out, and if I like the results you're hired." I showed her the door and reluctantly she left. I could understand her concern, but life is not always as we expect, and if she came back with some good ideas then maybe she could help me. I already had four other customers in the pipeline and I felt that I needed some serious help. That was just from the first few emails that I'd sent out – unbelievable!

I spent the afternoon on the phone with those customers and planned for the next three weeks ahead. One appointment after the other, no gaps or even time to have lunch; but if I wanted to succeed I had to work even harder. Eventually the guy I had called the week before came and installed a new signpost outside my office window: "GiGi – Personal Shopper – Fashion Consultant". And below that my phone number and website address.

What I liked most was that the banner was right there, in front of the Battersea Fashion Centre's face. People coming out of the shop would only have to look straight in front of them to see it. And all those people, frustrated by not having found what they were looking for, would see my shiny new sign and think it over. There you are, Jasper; let's see how you like it.

I had almost finished for the day when a text came in.

– *Hi, fancy having dinner with me tomorrow?*

That was Raffaele; we'd exchanged messages a couple of times but he'd never popped The Question yet.

- *Busy tomorrow. Big day with Natalie. What about the day after?*
- *Deal. Pick you up @ the office 7.30 PM?*
- *Sure. Not an Italian, please, I hate it.*
- *Ha, ha, ha. I'm stuffed then. See ya tomorrow. X x x*
- *Night x x x*

On second thoughts I could have said that I was free that very evening, but why should I come across as being too available? Sometimes it's better to let things flow at their own pace, find their own rhythm.

I didn't stay long in the office as the following day would be my final one with Natalie (furniture excluded). I actually had my car loaded with magazines and I would have possibly spent half of the night thinking about it and trying to figure out some ideas. I wasn't worried; I just wanted it to be perfect, to do something really nice for her.

I woke up very early in the morning. I spent most of the day scavenging for the right things for her, and then drove all the way to her place. That was a plus, in my line of work, getting paid to go shopping; shame I couldn't bring home all the stuff I was buying, but I've been there and it had almost bankrupted me. The temptation was hard to fight and eventually I bought something nice and outrageously expensive for myself as well. Hey, I was going on a date with the most gorgeous guy in town, so who could blame me?

With the car full to the brim, I couldn't wait to reach Natalie's and show her my findings.

"Oh my gosh!" she exclaimed when she opened the door. "I do hope you did some serious damage to my credit card."

"No peeking," I said, grabbing some of the bags and going towards the lounge.

"Are you kidding me? I've been waiting so long for this moment. This is Christmas coming early. Or late."

We went through the entire selection and she was ecstatic. It was only at around half past eight in the evening, after she'd tried at least half of what I had bought, that she relaxed a bit and invited me for dinner. We took her Bentley and she drove me to a French restaurant that was close to her place. A two-star Michelin place, they had grown to know her and her expensive tastes and they didn't complain when we showed up without notice.

Contrary to what they usually did, they sorted out a table for us on the spot, causing a hint of panic among the waiters, but otherwise unnoticed by the other guests. It was a treat from Natalie and I fully appreciated it.

She didn't believe in talking and eating at the same time and with food like that, I rather agreed with her. It was only when they served us the dessert that I risked mentioning the furniture.

"I've started working on it. And I should have something ready by next week."

"Are you sure you don't want to show me something upfront?" She was curious; she'd given me this task on purpose and was dying to see what I made of it.

"I am indeed; you'll either love it or hate it, but at least you know I'm putting all my effort into it. In the worst case I'd do it again – especially if you planned to take me for dinner here."

"Do you like it? The chef is friendly and we get along quite well; I met him in my gym a while ago. And he's cute."

"Must be a pandemic. I've just agreed to a date with a chef as well …" I didn't complete the sentence and Natalie was on me, asking for all the details. I also had to tell her about getting drunk and, although quite embarrassing for me, she found it very amusing.

"What do you plan to do with the old clothes?" I asked her with interest. "Charity shop?"

"I'm glad you asked. I had a thought last night;

tell me what you think. I'd like to give a funeral to some of the old clothes, in the garden; a real burial – that would make me feel I'm done with my past."

I gasped; I knew she was eccentric, but I'd never heard of anything like that before. I quite liked the idea, though. "I love it," I replied. "When do you want to hold the service?"

"Tonight, if you're up for it."

"Sure, why not? And the second half of your old wardrobe?"

"Oh, I have this friend who's doing a new series on ITV. We chatted a bit, you know – he's quite high up in the food chain, and he owes me a couple of favours. I'll donate the remainder of my clothes and a few other bits for a charity event they're doing. But the most important thing is that they're doing this new series, and I suggested you as a consultant. He saw the 'new me', and he didn't even flinch at the idea – quite the contrary. And they'll give you a mention in the credits: something like 'Clothes supervision by GiGi', and a reference to your website. OK, it's nothing huge – how many people really look at the credits? – but I've arranged for you to meet him and work out a deal for the other actors."

I gulped. That would be good exposure for me; imagine, being credited for sourcing clothes for a new series, working with real actors. The connections and the opportunities were endless.

We ended the dinner and drove back to her place.

"Come with me," she whispered, with a sadistic grin on her face and heading upstairs. We started putting some of the old clothes in a bag and slowly we brought them downstairs to the kitchen, by the back door. She opened a cupboard and got out a couple of pairs of oversized dungarees, far too big for either of us but which we wore nonetheless, and two pairs of wellies. With a torch in her hand she started searching in the vast garden until she was satisfied and then said, "You stay here." It was dark and I could barely see her walking in the general direction of the shed; a few thumping noises followed and then she reappeared with a pair of shovels and working gloves. She tossed a shovel to me. "Start digging the grave; I'll be back in a minute," she said, giggling like a teenager. I was flabbergasted; I'd thought she meant she'd bury her clothes in a figurative way, like at the bottom of the wardrobe. This was beyond belief! I pondered the situation for a moment and then I kicked the shovel in the ground; if we were going to make a mess, I'd better get started. The earth was soft from the previous days of rain and I could work quickly. I wondered for a moment if someone would see us, here in the garden, digging like a pair of tomb raiders, and would call the police.

"Ah good, you've started already," she said, depositing the bags nearby.

"Natalie, I'm not digging a six-footer here!" I complained; that would have taken the whole night.

"Not to worry, sweetheart: just deep enough to let all this stuff rot with the worms."

She started quarrying as well and after an hour we had to stop, because we were both quite tired but also because every few minutes we looked at each other and, without a word, we'd burst out laughing at what we were doing. I made a comment about the neighbours, and that also made her laugh out loud. "I'm going to put the kettle on," she said eventually. "Take a break."

I sat on the edge of the grave and let my legs float into the empty space; it was now almost a metre deep and perhaps it would have sufficed for the clothes. Natalie came back after a couple of minutes with the brews and we admired our work in silence. Eventually she was satisfied with the result and she tossed the lot in. Covering it up didn't take too long.

"I'd pay to see the face of your gardener when he discovers this."

Natalie burst out laughing again, and I had to sit down holding my belly at the thought of it.

"You can sleep in one of the spare rooms," she said, checking her watch, "but I'm afraid the gardener won't be around until the weekend. The neighbours are curious, though; this should keep them gossiping for quite a few days."

Eventually we were satisfied with our work. Even in the dark, you could see the bulge of freshly moved earth, which clearly resembled a grave. That would have made for a great episode of CSI.

With a flourish, Natalie picked up the empty bags, put away the shovels and announced it was time to have a nice hot toddy to take off the chill of the night air. I didn't argue, despite whisky not being my favourite. I have to say that the way she made it, with all the extras, it was delicious and I made a mental note to ask her for the recipe sometime.

We went to bed not long after, both exhausted.

CHAPTER 26

The next day, Natalie was kind enough to make me breakfast. She's up early every day these days, owing to her gruelling gym schedule and numerous social engagements. I thanked her for an eventful and enjoyable evening and hit the road. It was time to get to the office, as the number of clients requiring me to revisit their wardrobes was mounting up, and from them I was also receiving some extra referrals. I had to seriously start considering what I could do to get Ritchie back; how I could make it up to him.

I arrived at the office to find Erika, again sitting in the doorway. She was laden with magazines, with multi-coloured post-it notes sticking out of the top of them. I couldn't believe that she'd returned just one day after she'd been given her task, but, despite having far too much to do to keep my main business going and improving, I felt I owed it to Natalie to try to sort out her interior décor. Erika followed me into the office, sat down and waited. First order of the day was tea and so I asked her if she would mind making it, as I had to check the post and emails. If she really wanted a job, she'd do it. She was happy to, thankfully, as I wasn't particularly in the mood for small talk with someone who had just presented herself on my office doorstep – especially someone previously employed by Jasper and Lady Can'tLeaveHimAloneToLiveHisOwnLife! (blimey, the titles I'm giving her are getting longer and longer, but this one seemed appropriate; sorry about that!). I was busily going through emails, having already gone through the post, when Erika returned with the teas and sat down expectantly, like a dog waiting for a stick to be thrown. Just as she did, Ritchie came flying into the office yelling at the top of this voice, "Don't listen to her, don't listen to her; she's a spy!!!"

My jaw dropped and, before I could say "underpants", he continued, "She's working for Lady Whilsham and your/her ex!! You mustn't believe a word she says."

He then stopped in the middle of the floor, looking from one to the other of us and promptly closed his mouth. He hadn't expected Erika to be in the office when he burst in and was now starting to feel a little embarrassed and concerned. I took one look at Ritchie and I could see from the expression on his face that he was not joking; he was being damn serious. I then looked at Erika's face and saw such a shade of red spreading across it – clear evidence to me that Ritchie had to be telling the truth. I continued to look at her, hoping to stare a confession out of her, but she just sat there in silence. The look of complete shock on her face said it all, and the fact she had been discovered so early wouldn't have amused Lady StabYouInTheBack one bit.

Eventually I asked Ritchie to take a seat and elaborate on his proclamation, all the while leaving Erika to sit and listen. She just might have learned something from this. Ritchie couldn't tell me quickly enough. He'd been restocking shelves, in what he later referred to as the most mundane job he'd ever had, in this little boutique shop in Camden, when he had received a phone call from Harry. She had overheard a private conversation between her parents, talking about planning to have Erika work with GiGi and try to steal her ideas, her way of dealing with her customers. The Battersea Fashion Centre was doing OK, but they soon realised that they were missing the personalised experience that only someone like GiGi could give. They were good at business, they were good at cost-cutting; but they had finally understood that what they were missing was "a soul". Erika was the key to stealing that and trying to inject some fresh ideas into the mall, which otherwise would just become a low-cost shop.

Upon hearing that, Ritchie had to do something. He'd spent half that afternoon trying to convince his new boss to let him have the day off the following day, and when he refused he'd just walked out altogether, not caring about the consequences. He simply couldn't stand by and let this happen to me. As soon as Ritchie fell silent, I had one thing to say!

"Erika, I would like you to leave my office immediately and never return."

She then looked at me, dropped her head almost to her lap, or so it seemed, dropped the magazines she'd been holding and left, without a single word of explanation, apology or anything else. I sat there, so happy on the one part and disappointed on the other.

"I love you to bits!! Don't you ever try to leave me again," I said, all the while almost running from behind my desk to hug and kiss him.

We stood there in the middle of the office, crying in each other's arms and unable to speak for the joy of having finally found each other again. Eventually we sat on the sofa, and only after a few minutes were we able to talk to each other. Like magic, all the bitterness and hard feelings we'd both had during the past few weeks disappeared. I had my old Ritchie back and he, I hoped, had me.

"I feel like a worm for what I did to you.

Leaving and all – that wasn't right," he said, in tears. I could barely contain my emotion; on occasion when alone I'd almost cursed him, but I also knew he needed something solid, a regular income for his new life, and I couldn't honestly blame him for his decisions.

"Don't: you had your reasons, and I accept that."

"No – you don't get it. I spoke to Lillian yesterday, as I missed her house-warming party and she had a go at me. She told me about all the times you hadn't taken a salary, just to ensure I had one, and all the other bits. I couldn't have imagined it; I hated myself for the way I behaved, but at the same time I couldn't find the courage to face you."

Lillian – that big mouth. It was supposed to have been a secret, but at that point I didn't mind; just the opposite. If that's what it had taken to give a kick up the backside to Ritchie, I had to thank her and buy her a big dinner. And she'd introduced me to Raffaele. Bummer: I was in her debt, and I'd better do something before she started thinking I was an ungrateful bitch.

"Forget about all that; we have work to do." I explained about the job with Natalie, the new idea about the "Wardrobe Assessment Service" and how busy I was getting again.

"Are you taking me back?" he asked in disbelief.

"You're a partner, fifty/fifty – remember? You never left," I said and that cheered him up. "Maybe Erika did us a favour …" He looked at the folder and magazines that Erika had dropped on the floor and, while pondering an idea, he started shuffling through the pages. "Hmm … not really. As boring as her bosses … sorry about that."

"No need to apologise," I laughed. "Do you want to do the interior? Because if that's the case, I have to bring you up to speed on Natalie."

"Sure, but I want some of the old stuff as well, like that fashion assessment of yours. Just to diversify."

"Knock yourself out. Open the inbox and take your pick."

I went back to my office and started going through my emails. "I LOVE THE BOARD OUTSIDE THE WINDOW, BY THE WAY," Ritchie shouted from his desk. "MUST BE AN EYESORE FOR THE COMPETITION." I laughed aloud, but I was actually glued to a new email that had popped in that very moment.

Hello GiGi

My name is Osheena. Sorry to bother you, but I thought it was worth a try writing to you. I love fashion; I spend my days window-shopping and I've got more ideas than money. I'm trying to develop my own style and at the moment I think I'm getting somewhere, but I'm quite young and I feel I might need some direction. My parents do not understand me and always criticise me because I spend almost all my salary on clothes, saying that I should save for rainy days and all the sorts of things you might expect from sensible parents, and probably have heard yourself. Having said that, I feel there's a sense of satisfaction when all the things I buy fit together and, I know it's hard to explain, but I feel a better person when I can achieve the right combination of clothes, colours and accessories, to a point that I'm even more cheerful. I even think I'm better at work, with my friends, in my life. It might sound silly to you and I find it difficult to explain to you what's going on inside me, I can barely explain that to myself. Anyway, to cut a long story short, I would like to have some help, some direction, if I may ask.

I understand you deal with high-end fashion and most likely, I couldn't afford even a quarter of what you might have in mind. However, maybe we could find some sort of arrangement. I'd be happy to buy my own stuff and if it isn't high-end, so be it: I'm used to that. (It might sound silly, but I believe people shouldn't necessarily spend a fortune to look good.) Maybe I could pay your fees a bit every week?

I appreciate you might not be interested; as I said, it's a shot in the dark, but sometimes dreams are what makes the world go round, aren't they?

Cheers!
Osheena

I read the email twice, and I laughed out loud, to a point where Ritchie turned in my direction to see what was happening, as if maybe a comedian had entered the premises without him noticing and had started his gig.

So I wasn't alone in this world; there were actually other people out there like me, who felt the same way. Well, I did know I couldn't be the only one, but finding a sympathetic soul out there was indeed refreshing.

I looked at the couple of pictures she had attached and thought, "Hmmm … not that bad." Nothing in what she was wearing was expensive, but it worked. I actually had in my wardrobe that same skirt that she was wearing in her second picture, although I wore it with completely different clothes. And she was pretty, with a tall, slender figure, the kind that could wear almost anything and look good. She looked great. It didn't take me half a second to make my mind up: I would help her, and if that meant doing a pro bono, so be it. Ritchie was in too much of a good mood to complain, and business was picking up. So, *what the frock*, I thought; let's just do it.

Osheena

I'll be happy to collaborate with you on your "quest". Please come to my office either tomorrow afternoon (even out of hours, until 7.00 pm) or the following day, same time.

I'm sure we can figure something out.

Kind regards,
GiGi

I pressed the "send" button and a sense of relief permeated me. That was the difference from Jasper's outlet. We were working with people to make them feel better; they were in the business of selling stuff.

Another email came in a few seconds later.

Dear GiGi

I'm an executive in an investment bank in Canary Wharf. I came across your website by chance (actually my wife mentioned it, as she'd seen an advertisement in Battersea) and I thought that maybe you could help. I appreciate that what I'm going to ask isn't exactly your area of expertise, but I thought it was worth a try.

Maybe you could be of assistance in meeting us, where I could explain how to best fulfil our needs and point us in the right direction? That would be fantastic.

Looking forward to hearing from you,

Timothy Robertson

"RIIITCHIEEEE," I shouted.
"YES?"
"YOU TAKE THIS TIMOTHY GUY AND HIS WIFE! PRESENT YOURSELF AS ONE OF THE SENIOR PARTNERS AND GET HIM AN APPOINTMENT ASAP, PLEASE."

BLUE AND GREEN SHOULD NEVER BE SEEN!

"GOT IT. LEAVE IT TO ME."
Flippin' Nora: what a day.

CHAPTER 27

What a date!

I was expecting that a cook – sorry, a chef – would pick a very good restaurant for a first date. Hey, they're supposed to know their stuff, right? Raffaele took me completely by surprise instead, driving all the way down to Surrey; then from the M25 we went through country roads that became smaller and smaller until we reached this fabulous little restaurant, set in a very old cottage and surrounded by trees. If you didn't know it was there, you'd have missed it. No cars outside is usually a bad sign for a restaurant, but I had to reserve my judgement, at least for a while, before starting to share my point of view.

More panic overtook me when I realised the place was empty and the lights off. What was this going to be, a dinner with the ghosts?

And then Raffaele took out of his pocket an old key, the size of a mobile phone, opened the door and started searching for the light switch.

"Is this your place?" I asked him, stunned.

"I wish. No, it belongs to a friend of mine. Come inside," he said, after he'd managed to revive the place.

"Business must be tight."

"Ha, ha, ha – no, today it's closed. I asked if I could use his kitchen, and here we are. I didn't want to take you to a restaurant; I would have endorsed their job by doing that."

"Rather competitive, aren't you?" I said. In the meantime, I started looking around. The place was cool, old-style but properly done: low ceiling, Tudor walls where you could see the beams supporting the house. A huge inglenook fireplace was on the left and I could count just ten tables. This was indeed a cottage business, if you'll allow me the pun: but what a marvellous way to earn a living! A little place like that, old friends as customers, defined working hours and a passion instead of a job. I felt almost the same about what I was doing.

"So, your place will look like this?" I asked, thinking about the restaurant he was about to open.

"Not really, but this is a nice place nonetheless. Wait here a second." He went back to the car and returned with a bottle of red and a corkscrew. "Mind opening this while I unload the food from the car and get ready?"

"Not at all." I didn't have anything handy to remove the plastic at the top of the bottle, so I punched through it directly with the corkscrew. Sod it: I was going to be formal and all pretty and educated, if I had the chance.

He approached the fireplace, threw in some fire starters and kindling and pronto, in a few minutes the atmosphere was created.

"You have to help me with the cooking," he added, while he was still sipping his wine.

"Me? Sure; if you want fried eggs, or maybe beans on toast, I'm your girl. I can give you the recipe if you want."

"Ha, ha. Well, I'll pass on that offer, thanks. Nothing to worry about; I just need a sous-chef to help me with the preparation. I can finish the rest off."

"A sous-chef? Sounds like either your little personal slave who peels the potatoes and chops the onions, or someone you can bark orders to at will."

"No, that would happen if you were working in my kitchen as a regular. With guests, I'm worse. So, what do you think?"

"Well … in this case: yes, chef!"

"Atta girl! Give me a minute to unload the rest." He went back to the car and I sipped my wine, mesmerised by the orange colours of the fire and the ruby reflection in the wine. He returned bringing a couple of boxes, balancing one on top of the other. I closed the door behind him, placed my glass on a table near the fireplace and grabbed one of the boxes. "Here, let me give you a hand."

"Thank you."

Blimey, it was heavy; what did he have in mind to feed me – a goose? I followed him and we started unpacking.

"Starter is going to be Singapore chilli crab, and for main, quail cooked three ways, with mushrooms and celeriac purée."

"Sounds complicated." I started worrying; I was definitely out of my comfort zone.

"Oh, it isn't! Here, take this." He handed me a crab. I mean, not like the ones you find in the supermarket, but already … oh my gosh, how do you say? "Peeled"? Nah, you don't peel a crab; you take off the hard stuff. Was there even a term for such a thing? He gave me a hammer and for a moment I stood there stock still, not knowing what to do. Surely, he didn't want me to kill the poor animal.

"They're already dead," he said, as if reading my mind. He passed me an apron and then started bashing the thing. It seemed easy; I did the same, and the beast slipped away as I hit it on a corner, and fell on the ground. Shit! What about a bit of cooperation, you little monster? We laughed; him from enjoyment, and me from embarrassment. I picked it up and I was ready to murder the thing again (or die trying) when Raffaele showed a bit of compassion and helped me out.

"Here, hold it this way and hit right here." He was right behind me and was holding my hands, showing me what I was supposed to do. For a second I thought about missing on purpose, just to not let him get away. It was reassuring being there with his arms around me.

"Hey! I did it! I smashed the thing." I was covered by pieces of broken shell and salty water, which hit me in the face. An apron had definitely been a good idea.

"OK: now, with a spoon you take out all this white meat and then the brown. Then open the claws and take the meat out with this." He passed me a little metal fork. I was just halfway when he had already finished his. He was already chopping chilli, making pastes and broths by the time I'd finished my task. Next for me was chopping the coriander and cutting the ginger.

He told me about his past when, in his early twenties, he'd gone to Paris to learn and had the chance of working with this two-Michelin-star chef. I gathered it was a hard life, being busy when everybody else was free and free only when all the other cooks were. He used to play football at night, in the main square where the restaurant was – often at two in the morning – with the other cooks and people working there. He told me about his passion, what made him decide that was going to be his life and how one day he would do his own thing. I recognised by listening to him that cooking could be a form of art, which I'd never realised before, I was stuck at judging food as bad, good and excellent, but had never for a moment stopped and thought about the process – designing a plate, mixing the right flavours in the right amounts – and I was fascinated by this new experience Raffaele was showing me. While cooking, he occasionally stopped what he was doing and said, "Try this," almost shoving a spoonful of food into my mouth. "What do you think?"

Everything was delicious; no, it was better than that. Being part of that creative process of taking raw food, mixing it together in the right way, was something for which I'd have been grateful to Raffaele forever. He made me discover a new world, a parallel universe.

Dinner was ready and we took the starters into the dining room. Something special happens if you cook with someone you like (and you don't kill each other in the process); there's a communion of feeling that you share and that you can hardly experience in any other way. Feeding is a basic process, but the process of preparing the food is not. I would have loved to be able to quote Hugh Jackman in the film *Kate and Leopold*, but those lines eluded me. Something about a meal taking time and a lot of reflection.

What an experience!

We talked a lot about ourselves, about our dreams and what we would do in reality. I felt close to him in a way I'd never felt with anyone else before (except maybe Ritchie, but that didn't count), and I could see Raffaele was feeling the same way. There was something there and I only hoped it would be as good as I imagined it could be. I needed someone like him on my side; talking was easy, and so was laughing. He had a funny, wicked sense of humour that I didn't get the first time we'd been together.

We didn't make dessert; Raffaele thought I would get bored if he pushed me too much into his world. Honestly, I wasn't and I'd have spent the whole night, sitting there, or cooking with him. He had prepared a cake while at home, and for the occasion we opened another bottle; this time it was a sweet wine. It was when we went back to the kitchen that we kissed, just when we were ready to cut a couple of slices of that beautiful, rustic cake. Our eyes locked for a second too long and we both knew what would happen next. I don't remember (and I didn't care) who made the first move; in a matter of seconds we were in each other's arms, searching our bodies and kissing passionately. For a brief moment, I realised that it was our first date, and I panicked. What would he think of me? To hell with all that; I counted the day spent painting Lillian's house as our first date. Nothing to worry about, then.

And frankly, if you were in the arms of a man as dishy as Raffaele, you'd have stopped counting as well. Believe me.

Fortunately the restaurant also had some spare rooms upstairs. We spent the night making love until, both exhausted, sleep finally took us.

CHAPTER 28

Osheena came into the office a couple of days later, and so did Timothy and his wife a few minutes after that. Ritchie had practically finished the interior design for Natalie and, for a moment, it looked as if our business was flourishing again.

Osheena was an attractive black girl in her mid-twenties, with straight hair and a contagious smile. I recognised her from the pictures she'd sent me previously, of course, but I could also appreciate what she was wearing. I saw a "little GiGi" in her straight away, with a desire and an objective in her mind but a lack of funds to realise them. Hopefully she hadn't been through a "credit card" phase like I had. I made a mental note to ask her later. She looked around, maybe trying to get a better understanding of what we were really doing here.

"Hi – I'm GiGi." I introduced myself promptly, and the smile on her face made me feel that this was going to be a great day.

"Osheena. Nice to meet you."

"Come to my office. Oh, I forgot: would you like a cup of coffee?"

"Just if you're having one yourself," she answered.

We went to the kitchen and the interview process started.

"So, how did you find us?"

"I went to visit the Battersea Fashion Centre and I saw you advertisement. That made me curious, so I went online and did some research."

"Our website is quite basic," I said sheepishly. I'd discussed that matter umpteen times with Ritchie and we promised each other that we should have done something. Word of mouth was great and gave us plenty of business, but at some point, we should have scaled it up. The only IT stuff we had was the mobile app, and even that we kept quite secret, for our customers' eyes only.

"I realised that. But I found there's quite a buzz about this mysterious woman helping people to find their own style. Blogs are starting to talk about this strange woman, but they haven't made the connection yet."

"And you did." That got me thinking – maybe there was an avenue there that we hadn't exploited yet.

"Yeah, I thought so. It's amazing what I've seen. You know, there was a post on one of the most important blogs and it went on for pages and pages. Someone even claimed it was an urban legend, a conspiracy theory. Quite amusing."

We went to my office with our cuppas and sat on the sofa, like two old friends who had finally found each other after years apart.

"So, what do you do for a living?"

"I have a job in IT; I'm a programmer. Quite boring stuff, if you ask me. I mean, I love the job, don't get me wrong, but it's a multinational company, all corporate and no room for imagination. A bit frustrating, if you ask me. I also work in a bar twice a week, to raise some more cash. I never seem to have enough and I have expensive tastes."

I knew exactly what she meant, but something in what she said got me thinking …

She went on, "I know I probably couldn't afford your services. What I read from the blogs is that you are really high-end fashion and …" I stopped her mid-sentence with a wave of my hand. My fees were expensive, but that was just because I happened to work with people that could afford it.

"Are you good at your job?" I suddenly asked.

"Excuse me?" she looked surprised.

"Are you good at programming and doing your job?"

"I'm the best."

"OK, then this is what we can do. Service and wardrobe are on me; and you build me the very best website you can think of – something unique, that you can throw all your imagination into." It was a punt, but sometimes you have to follow your gut instinct, don't you? Even that *Dragon's Den* guy says that sometimes you invest in the people and not the idea. Well, that was the case for me. Osheena was ... "very investable."

"I ... I suppose I could ..." She was shocked; for a moment she looked at me as if I was joking. Then I could see from the look in her eyes that her mind was spinning, starting to formulate ideas. I was right: I'd made the right decision and she wouldn't disappoint me. "Yes, I'd be glad to," she said finally. "I ... you'll be amazed! And if you don't like what I create, I'll pay off every penny, I promise."

We were just shaking hands when Ritchie came into the room.

"GiGi, would you mind coming with me for a moment?" There was a strange look on his face. I excused myself and followed him into the open space directed towards the other room, where Timothy and his wife were ... arguing? "What's going on, Ritchie? Talk to me ..." I said, hurrying him up, since we were almost at the door.

"I'll let you find out for yourself," he replied. He opened the door and introduced me to the couple as the senior partner.

"I told you this wasn't a good idea," said the

woman who I presumed was the wife.

"How can I be of assistance?" I asked, sitting at the far end of the table and opening my notepad.

"Well … as I tried to explain to your partner," he said, pointing at Ritchie, "we'd like some consultancy in respect of my wife's shoes …"

"He's a fetishist!" the woman added, screaming, "It's a psychiatrist we need to see, not a fashion consultant!"

I looked at Ritchie as if he could provide an explanation that never came. "OK, Mr Robertson: why don't we take a step back and you explain exactly what you're looking for?"

"Well … I like shoes …" he started saying.

"You're a fetishist. Say it out loud – that's what you are," screamed the wife.

"Please go on," I urged, hoping she wouldn't interrupt further.

"You know … this is embarrassing … as I said, I like feet in a nice pair of shoes. I won't go into details, but … it excites me. I feel a sense of desire when … and my wife won't do it."

I looked at the wife, who was definitely raging, and without being noticed I tried to have a peek at her shoes. Ritchie was nonchalantly walking towards the window, but I knew only too well that he was trying to do the same. He looked at me and, without being seen by either of them, he put a finger in his mouth as though he was trying to puke. I almost laughed out loud in front of them, and I tried to look at my notes.

"Madam, you're the first woman I've ever met to refuse a pair of expensive shoes."

She looked uncomfortable and tried to justify herself. "I like being comfortable."

I bet you do, I thought; I can smell ballerinas from where I'm sitting. If there was a passion killer, that was it: well above pyjamas with pugs on and fluffy, peluche slippers.

"Would it be agreeable to be a bit uncomfortable just at some times of the day? For example, when going out for dinner? Or maybe at home, twice a week?"

"I suppose I could make an effort." She knew she was going to be cornered, but she was also gaining something in the process. Hubby was a banker, after all.

"So would you like to have a look at some samples my partner here has in stock?" It was an outright lie, and I hoped Ritchie thought about that "on his feet". He did. He excused himself and came back with a ton of shoes, stolen from my personal office wardrobe. He apologised, saying he had no way of knowing the correct size; but they were the right size.

Lady wife was trying on a nice Italian pair and I could almost see tears of joy in the husband's eyes.

My job here was done; Ritchie would follow through with that.

CHAPTER 29

Money started pouring in. We finally sorted out Natalie's house and she was one of the happiest clients I'd ever seen; most importantly, she wasn't ashamed now to bring a date home and be scared of giving the wrong impression. The old Victorian, all-wood style that would have suited an old granny had changed to the modern, refreshing, new style that Ritchie had sorted out, single-handed. We both received the biggest bunch of flowers we'd ever seen in our lives as a thank you. Natalie was also dating now; there was this Tyrone guy, in her words a hotter version of Denzel Washington (if that's even possible), who owned a software company near Winnersh and who she'd met in the same posh gym that she went to. I was wondering if, one day, she would find the courage to tell him about the "body" we'd buried in the garden.

She had connections and organised a visit from *Country Life* magazine and, if I knew her, would manage to have her place featured as the main article in one of the following issues. People asked about her transformation and she pointed them in our direction, which made Ritchie and I even busier, to the point where we had to devise another way of classifying our clients. Now, in addition to the Silver, Gold and Platinum, which was our internal way of assessing the customers, we had the Advanced, Premium and Ultimate offerings.

Advanced was a short assessment made in a couple of days, with suggestions on style and follow-up visits to the shops with our clients to ensure that they stuck to our recommendations. The Premium was our bread and butter, what we had usually done up to that point, while the Ultimate would be the ones who would push the boundaries – special cases where we would do pretty much anything the clients could throw at us.

We started struggling before long and it seemed evident we needed more bodies, but we decided to park that issue for a few more days. Ritchie would start making enquiries with his friends, in a hush-hush way, and I was to do the same. Blimey: we needed to seriously think about that. Once the new website went online, matters could become even worse and it's never a good idea to turn down potential customers.

That's the problem when the business side of your life is going well: you put a lot of energy into it and little remains for your private life. What saved me was that Raffaele was also busy in sorting out his restaurant, which was almost finished, but soon we would have to face the issue at hand. The reality was that there was little overlapping in our lives. We spent as much time together as we could, and one day I also took a break from my job and accompanied him to the countryside, sourcing fresh food for his restaurant.

"So, where are we going today?" I asked eagerly. It was almost six in the morning and I was still half asleep, whilst Raffaele had been up for almost an hour and was becoming a little twitchy. He was used to getting up even earlier to go to markets and farms; for him we were already a couple of hours late.

"We have four farms to visit in Surrey and Kent; if the food is of good quality, then we can make a deal for supply."

The first farm was in Kent, not far from Edenbridge. We drove through the village and passed some lovely Tudor houses on both sides of the road. I was glued to the window, trying not to let anything pass by unnoticed. A beautiful house just outside the village caught my attention, with a massive willow tree just at the front. The place looked the epitome of a quiet and relaxed life –

something that occasionally I craved.

"Look at that one," I said to Raffaele. He slowed the car down and was silent for a moment.

"The countryside here is beautiful. I've always been in big cities and it still amazes me how lucky people are to live in a place like this."

"That's also a dream of mine," I added, although I knew that at this point in my life it would probably remain a dream. "Coming home and finding a lit fireplace, maybe a dog greeting me when I enter the door, and enjoying a glass of wine in the quiet surroundings of my garden." I could have added that probably I wouldn't have minded coping with a couple of screaming kids, but we hadn't dated for long, Raffaele and me, so I was a bit skittish about mentioning that.

"Or a couple of kids ambushing you behind the door," he added. I laughed out loud, as we were thinking about a very similar image in our minds, but Raffaele took it the wrong way, as if I was making fun of his dream. I noticed he went quiet and kept his focus on the road ahead of us.

"I didn't mean to laugh," I then added. "I was thinking the very same thing, although I didn't spell it out." I hoped that would have been enough.

"I could live in one of those," he said, pointing to a lovely seventeenth-century manor house with red bricks and a lawn in the front garden that was so perfect it could have been a carpet.

"Yeah, I could settle for something like that as well." House spotting was a favourite pastime of mine whilst I was driving around visiting my clients. I would look at houses I liked and dream of one day having something like that. With a swimming pool.

We passed the mansion and, after a mile, we had to turn onto a small country lane, wide enough for just one car. Good thinking that we'd taken Raffaele's car, a four by four, because the road soon became just two furrows in the grass and mud. Eventually we reached the farm. A border collie came to greet us, followed by the owner, shouting; she was a woman in her mid-sixties.

"Sorry about Nelson," she said, "he wants to greet everybody and today he's as muddy as hell."

"No problem," said Raffaele, patting the dog, which went belly-up straight away.

"Look at you; you are a mess," the woman said to our new best friend. "Go away, shoo."

Raffaele introduced himself and the restaurant he now proudly owned. The woman's name was Julia. They spoke for a while about the farm, their produce and other things I didn't quite catch. The good news was that the farm could provide a good quantity of fresh lamb and beef. Raffaele struck up a deal on all the oxtails she could put her hands on, bought about a hundred pounds of meat the woman kept in a fridge in the office, and they sorted out details about delivery and quantities. He would have to try the meat first, but he was happy with what he'd seen after Julia had shown us around. Good thinking by Raffaele about bringing wellies, which I hadn't thought of.

And off we went on our next quest for fresh produce in the countryside.

"Oxtail?" I asked, incredulous.

"Cooked properly, it's delicious. In this country, most people buy meat in supermarkets and they always get the same cuts. The tail is a cheap cut, but nonetheless delicious; you should try it." I was unconvinced, but I trusted Raffaele.

"You know what?" he added. "Why don't we organise a dinner with some friends this weekend? I will convert you to oxtail. And if I don't prepare the best dish you've ever eaten in your life … well … you pick the reward."

"Oh, it's a bet?"

"Why not?"

"Deal. Careful there, though, because I have a lot of imagination on how to get compensated."

"I guess you do," he said, with a gleam in his eye.

I didn't mind driving through the countryside with Raffaele. Visiting farms wasn't my cup of tea, but I loved being with him; and if that was what it was going to take to spend some further time together, so be it. We tried the other way around – doing shopping – a couple of times, but after an hour or two he started walking behind me like a zombie, with glassy eyes, and I soon realised shopping wasn't for him. We also bought a couple of walkie-talkies and made an agreement: he accompanied me for one hour doing shopping, after which he'd find a nice café in the area where he could have a beer and read a book while I was in shops doing my thing. Once in a while we got in touch.

"How's the shopping going? Over."

"Almost done (which translated meant at least half an hour more, in my warped shopping time). Over. Where are you? Sorry I said 'over' before it was over. Over."

"Pub on the main street. Sitting outside. Over."

"See you in a bit. Over."

Those little toys had a range of a couple of miles, and even if we looked as if we were a couple of spies (or security guards), we didn't care. It was a way like any other of being together without too much pain. A short shopping trip on my side or a too long one on his: the right compromise.

Although exhausted by the trip and driving all day visiting farms, we still had the energy to go to my place or his and have a great dinner.

That – and making love.

CHAPTER 30

How do you recognise true love?

I didn't have an answer for that. I'd had my share of boyfriends in the past and with some of them I had thought I was in love. Despite that, there was always something missing: a detail, a feeling in the gut that I wasn't completely happy. It's in my nature to be a perfectionist and, on more than one occasion, I let slip on matters that otherwise I would not have done.

As an example – the right level of attention that I needed: and I needed a lot. I don't mean having someone around me all the time, like a sort of servant; I mean someone to share interests with and who makes that unexpected gesture that surprises you occasionally. I could hardly express what I needed, and so it was even more difficult trying to talk about it, but so far Raffaele was fitting the role. He had his own space but, at the same time, he had that ability to get me involved that had been lacking in all my previous relationships. For once, I could feel we were doing things together: not all the time, but when our lives crossed and more often than I expected. I took an interest in his restaurant without stepping on his toes, as we did when we went farm-hunting, and he did the same with my work.

At that point we spent almost every evening at his place. Well, I would say I'd all but moved in, if it wasn't for the little, ickle detail about the humongous wardrobes I had at my place. Blimey, I needed to live in a warehouse to accommodate those.

I woke up that morning and the bed was empty, although I could still feel the warmth of his body under the sheets, and a hint of his aftershave. I already missed him. How he had the energy to make love the whole night and still be able to carry on with his morning duties was a mystery to me. I was still shattered. A rose and a handwritten note were on the bedside table … where had he found a rose?

"GiGi, had to go to the restaurant for the final changes. I'm still nervous about the opening, which is approaching fast. I left some breakfast for you; just turn the oven on for fifteen minutes at a hundred and eighty degrees. Love you loads. X x x, Raf."

I stretched and just the thought of food started waking me up, but I was in desperate need of a cuppa first. I was slowly getting out of bed when the phone rang.

"GiGi!" It was Ritchie. "They're shutting us down!" I could feel the panic in his voice.

"Whatever are you talking about?" I asked. I looked at my watch and it was already nine in the morning. I hadn't heard the alarm.

"The Council is here and they're claiming they've had complaints – hazardous stuff and other things that I don't have half a clue what they are."

"And they want us to close the premises?" I couldn't connect yet; I wasn't there and I hardly understood what the complaints could be about. We were working in an office, not in a shop. People rarely visited us.

"OK, do it this way. I'm going to grab a quick shower and then come straight to the office. You call Tom in the meantime and see what he can do: at least he'll understand what all this fuss is about."

I hung up the phone and my legs were shaking. The new website had gone online just a couple of days previously and the phone had started to ring non-stop. Think, GiGi, think! We could still work remotely and visit the clients in the pipeline, but we were also expecting people to show up at the door. And we'd decided to hire, so potential candidates, due to come that week for an interview, would find us closed. Oh dear: that wasn't a nice business card –coming for an interview and seeing that your new potential employer had been shut down.

Forget the shower; I jumped into my clothes and ran to my car as if I was running for my life. which, in some respects, I was.

I was driving towards London when my mother called.

"Hello, GiGi: how are you doing, my dear?"

"Mum, I have an emergency at the office," I answered. There are moments in life when you hate technology, and in my case at that very moment I hated the hands-free kit I'd had installed in the car.

"Oh – what's happened then?" she asked, as if she was enquiring about the weather. No curiosity, no sense of urgency. I was experiencing a drama and she wanted to do the conversation thing.

"I don't know; the Council wants to close our office. We've had complaints … hazards … I don't know the details yet."

"I told you so. Starting your own business isn't easy. There are all those laws and regulations that need to be checked. I remember Cousin Peter, when he decided to open that restaurant in Devon …"

"Mum," I interjected, "I'm not a restauranteur. We have an office."

"And nonetheless offices have their own rules. Do you have a fire extinguisher?" OH-MY-GOSH!!!

Now she'd started with one of her tirades.

"Yes, of course we have. One in each room, actually."

"Maybe it's that kitchen of yours. You know, sometimes offices have just a coffee machine or a kettle. If you have a full kitchen you might have to follow different rules," she continued. That was what pissed me off most; she didn't have a clue and still she was ready to give advice.

"I assure you we washed all the dishes yesterday evening."

"Don't be sarcastic, young lady. I'm just trying to help." No, she wasn't.

"Mum, do you know the details of why they're shutting us down?" I asked, almost on the verge of shouting at her. I was dodging white vans, which were driving as if they were at Brands Hatch, and I was struggling to negotiate traffic lanes; I didn't have time for this.

"No, but common sense …"

"I'll call you back, OK? I'm driving."

"As you prefer – I was just trying to be helpful …"

"Bye."

It took me almost an hour to reach the office and when I entered the door Tom was already there, talking to one of the officers. Ritchie took me aside and filled in the gaps. "It was Jasper," he whispered in my ear.

WHAT?

"Why did that bastard make a complaint? And

about what?" I was fuming. We weren't even in the exact same line of business; why would he take revenge like that?

"We have too much stuff in the office. Shoes, samples – all sorts of things. We've had two complaints: one is for a fire hazard and the second is on the safety side. People could trip on things and get hurt," he explained to me. Tom is handling it brilliantly.

"I still don't understand …" At that point Tom finished with the officer, who went on his way. Finally, we had a chance of learning what this was all about.

"Nothing to worry about, GiGi." He explained how a Jasper Barnes had logged a complaint about the premises. Usually they ignored things like that or, at most, the Council would send out an inspector. It was rather unusual that they came out straight away to close an office. The papers had been filed the previous evening and someone was on our doorstep that very morning.

"You have a powerful enemy, GiGi," Tom added. "He had to pull some strings to force the Council to act so quickly. I don't have any evidence, but I suspect someone was paid to speed things up. Be careful there."

"Tom, I don't know how to thank you. I mean, coming here straight away like that and sorting things out."

"Don't mention it," he added, as if for him it was just a walk in the park "I found it a nice diversion from my routine! And I'm sure Lillian will come up with something."

We laughed, although Ritchie's and mine were mostly signs of relief rather than amusement. Still, we needed to understand why Jasper had gone to all this trouble. Tom left soon afterwards, after we'd shared a cup of coffee, and we promised to make up for his help.

"So why d'you think he did it?" Ritchie's question was the million- dollar one.

"Not a clue."

"Maybe jealousy? We're becoming successful, and you have a new boyfriend. People like him don't like rejections."

I pondered that for a moment, but it didn't make any sense. The answer came that very afternoon, when I met with Osheena for our shopping rendezvous.

"Of course he tried to stop you," she said, as if it was the most obvious thing in the world – but I still didn't get it.

"Mind explaining?" I asked, while we were trying on a pair of Jaeger footwear.

"Did you see the statistics on your web page, and the following you're getting on the blog?"

To be honest, I hadn't. I'd seen the website, and it was a piece of art, but when it was a matter of going into details, I was lost. Osheena also volunteered to write a few articles for the blog. I just gave her a few notes, but she'd elaborated on those and made three or four very good articles out of them.

"Ermm …"

"Don't you get it?" she added passionately "People are following your blog. They made the connection between the mysterious fashion woman and you. Well, actually I made more than one hint on the blog, to be honest. GiGi, you can shift people from one place to another."

She was talking gibberish; I was afraid to ask.

"Shifting, GiGi. You can set trends! If you say something is cool, people will go and check it out, and if you say something is uncool, people will wonder."

I started to grasp what she was saying. "You mean that there's a wider audience out there, who care about what I'm saying?"

"It's more than that. You've already more than forty thousand people following you. You could make the fortune of a shop just by mentioning it."

"Or the opposite?" I asked tentatively.

"Yes, even that." Everything was so clear for Osheena; she was actually working in that sector and she definitely knew what she was talking about. And I loved her passion.

"Forty thousand people?" I said aloud. The sound of it was astounding; I could barely believe it. Suddenly I had an idea.

"Wait here; I have a phone call to make." I went out of the shop and frantically started searching for the number on the screen. When eventually I came back I had more than one idea in my head.

"Osheena, I have a proposal. What about dumping that extra work of yours in the restaurant and being paid for managing the website and the blog?"

"Are you kidding me?" she said, almost screaming with joy. A shop assistant looked at us with fierce eyes, as if we were disturbing the quiet and atmosphere in the shop. "I'd even ask you to work full time for me, but I can't match the stability of a job in a multinational company …" I couldn't complete the phrase: Osheena jumped to her feet and put her arms around me, almost lifting me off the ground.

"I'd have done it for nothing. Are you serious – I mean, you really want me to take care of the website and the blog?"

"Why not? You've done a perfect job so far. It's just …" Again I couldn't complete the sentence; but in that very moment I realised Ritchie and I had made the right decision in offering her the position. We both loved her and what she'd done for us already. It was only fair to give her a chance to follow her dream. Were we a bunch of dreamers, as Mother would say?

I didn't think so.

CHAPTER 31

Apologising wasn't my cup of tea, but that was what I had to do for Raffaele. Not that he asked for it, but after he'd seen that the breakfast he'd prepared with such tender loving care was still in the oven, untouched, he hadn't been pleased.

We were both nervous (OK, to be honest, I was the nervous one! He was as cool as a cucumber) about the restaurant opening, and because Ritchie and I were seriously expanding our own business. The interview process was taking for ever and we couldn't seem to find the right candidates. Some people just wanted a job (by all means, that's a good motivation, but we needed more than that), others had previously worked in shops or department stores. The latter had good knowledge of brands, but putting everything together was a different matter. In the end, we had all sorts of people who thought they had a style. They were the ones who were the most similar to my partner and me, but with variety and imagination come the risks. The question of how to source additional workforce was wide open. We managed to hire a friend of Ritchie's, but that was all. We thought of hiring a recruiter, but we couldn't even agree on the right parameters for judging a candidate. What a mess.

We would know if someone was right by talking to that individual – but we couldn't afford to interview half of London.

We promised each other we'd have to discuss it further, but we didn't; so the elephant stayed in the room and we just kept ignoring it, overloading ourselves as a result. I knew I was the one who should have done something, but I managed to procrastinate. I can be good at that, when I want.

"Numaka Investment Bank: how can I help you?" answered the voice on the other end of the phone.

"Good morning, Griselda Griswald speaking; may I talk to Mr Robertson, please?"

"I'll connect you to his assistant; please hold the line." The more important people were, the more filters you had to pass through.

"Mr Robertson's office: good morning. Unfortunately Mr Robertson is in a meeting; may I take your name and a message?"

"Sure, I'm Griselda Griswald; I'm calling …"

"Hold on, I'll pass you through."

I just had time to listen to the initial three seconds of Beethoven's ninth symphony when Timothy answered.

"GiGi, nice to hear from you; how are things going? Do you need a loan?" He was definitely joyful and happy to hear from me.

"No, nothing like that. I hope I'm not disturbing you."

"Me? Nah, I was in one of those bull meetings that suck the life out of you and nothing gets done. We're floating an IT company and we had to look busy and interested." I was glad I'd caught him in a busy moment; I was starting to wonder how he would have reacted on a quiet, boring day.

"Oh, I almost forgot," he continued, as if he was on a roll, "I have to thank your colleague, Ritchie. He did amazingly with that shoe task of mine, and the way he convinced my wife? Astonishing. Think, now not only does she wear those amazing pieces, but she also allows me to give her a foot massage …"

"Timothy …" I tried to interject.

"… And our sex life? Such an improvement. She walks up and down the house, firstly with a pair of fabulous pumps on, and then …"

"Timothy …"

"Oh, sorry, what did you say?" Finally I'd managed to get his attention.

"Timothy, too many details, but thank you."

"Oh …yes … sure. What were you calling about, then?"

"I have this friend of mine – well, actually my boyfriend – who's opening a restaurant down in Surrey. I was wondering if you and your wife would like to be there for the opening on the twenty-third?"

"I'd be glad to be. What's the address?"

I gave him the details, exchanged pleasantries and we promised each other to get in touch again. He asked if he could add a couple of friends, an important stockbroker and his wife, and I said sure – why not? I'd have to inform Raffaele straight away for good measure.

Next on the list was Natalie. "How are you, darling? News is that you're climbing up the ladder," she said, straight off the bat.

"Hey, Nat! Things are going great – even better than we'd envisaged. We're struggling to manage."

"That's what happens when the word gets out there nowadays. You know, all the social media; you can't control any more how things happen and how quickly. I'll have to make an appointment now to talk to you!"

"Are you kidding? After all the skeletons in the cupboard we've shared?" I laughed.

"Good, because I have some friends to send your way. Now that the cat's out of the bag, and they know I'm a friend of "The GiGi" whom everybody's talking about on the internet, people are starting to ask favours. "

"About favours …" I said tentatively, as I always took pride in doing things myself, counting on my own energy and effort, and asking favours wasn't something that fitted well with my character. However, I was doing this for Raffaele, so it made me feel less bad. I continued, "My boyfriend is opening his own restaurant on the twenty-third. It's in Surrey, but I was wondering if you'd like to come along."

"I'd be glad to. A restaurant, you say? The food columnist in the *Mail* is actually a friend of mine; we went to school together. Mind if I bring her along? That would be stunning publicity."

A critic? I wasn't sure about that; I mean, I'd never discussed critics with Raffaele, but for sure this was an opportunity, right? He was an amazing cook – pardon, chef – so the right publicity would be welcome, I thought. Shit: now it was too late to take the invitation back; if I said anything Natalie would think I was inviting her to dine in a fast-food place.

"Not a problem, Nat. I'll text you the address. So how's the rest?"

"I have a boyfriend now, too," she said, giggling like a teenager.

"The one from the gym? The Denzel Washington look-alike?"

"You reckon he looks like him?" she asked, puzzled.

"He's definitely hot like him."

"Well, that's the one, then – the hottest guy in Berkshire. I'll send you the details of those friends of mine. Treat them nicely," she joked.

"I will. OK, catch you later."

"See you on the twenty-third; looking forward to it. 'Bye."

At that point, I didn't know whether I was going to be a hero or a villain. But it wouldn't take long to find out.

CHAPTER 32

More customers.

Osheena was under training; however, she was a natural. She worked with both Ritchie and me and she understood exactly what we were doing and how; now the question was, would she be able to put her spin on things, adding her own personality? In theory the answer was "yes", as I trusted my instincts, but plans don't always go as expected, and I knew something about that! We needed another couple of people at least to keep up the pace, but we were reluctant to hire. First we wanted to be sure that we could sustain the growth; no point in hiring people when you can't guarantee them a future, and not fair either. But I had an idea.

I could hire some consultants myself and, if they were working within my guidelines, ethic and style, perhaps we had a way out of working twenty hours a day. We also needed a secretary; getting emails and phone calls was all fine and dandy, but that left us rather disorganised. We could cope when it was just Ritchie and me, but now with Osheena and Jacob, Ritchie's new recruit, things were becoming more complicated.

My little sister could maybe give a hand now that she'd finished university and was waiting to find a job, and for other potential candidates I started contacting a few of the bloggers Osheena had put me in touch with. That, at least, was the outcome of a little brainstorming I'd had the previous day with Ritchie. Hey, with some of them, we had similarities and maybe I could strike up some collaboration. What better than putting into practice what you're actually suggesting, on your own blog, with real, paying customers? For those not just interested in chatting, it was the chance to put their ideas into practice. At a later stage, they could either choose to remain or, if they preferred, they could start their own business. I wasn't afraid of competition and, let's be honest, London alone has more than 8 million people; there's plenty of space for a few more consultants.

Of course, my aim was to retain them, but I had little control over what decisions they might make in future. I'll spare you all the details about the training hours we put in for Osheena and Jacob, and the nights up in the office, sustaining ourselves only by means of coffee and takeaways – but it was tough.

I hadn't seen Raffaele in days and I was missing him. Well, work was also the excuse for not having told him about the critic Natalie was taking along for the opening. I'm good at procrastinating; I can do it for days and weeks, keeping on delaying things to a later time until I reach a point when a matter becomes unavoidable.

"Rachel," – I was calling my sister – "are you still looking for that elusive job?"

"Hello, Sis. Indeed; how're you doing?"

"I'm grand. Business is flourishing and I'm working twenty hours a day." It was not actually that good when you have to just work all the time, but I didn't really want to complain.

"My internship went belly-up. Six months spent doing Excel spreadsheets and cleaning up after the mess of six sales people, and now that I have a degree, they're shrinking – or downsizing, or whatchamacallit. Anyway, I'm stuck doing a bar job and sending out CVs, waiting for someone to recognise my raw talent." Rachel was in good spirits. Excellent.

"I might have a proposition for you. I'm looking for someone to look after a few headless chickens, me included, doing some secretarial work, and maybe helping out with the website and the blog. Whatever you want to grab, you're welcome to.

You'd still have time for interviews and your own stuff. And we can pay!" I said, all in one breath. Oh dear – maybe I did sound a bit too desperate, but she was my sister; she needed something else to put on the CV and … I needed her.

"I suppose I could. When would I start?"

"The sooner the better. You could tag along tomorrow and I can show you how things work."

"Sounds like a plan. Are you seeing someone?" she asked unexpectedly. Usually she didn't get too involved in my business, and I was glad that for once she had demonstrated some interest.

"I'm trying to. Yes, I've got a boyfriend now: a nice one. But I'm too busy to even get a chance to see him properly." It was true, and I felt guilty about that. Business and love don't go well together and I was torn apart by the two. Of course I wanted to spend more time with Raffaele, but at the same time we'd never been so busy before and things were really picking up. I had a chance to succeed at what I loved; I had responsibilities towards the other people working with me. Things would settle down eventually, I was sure of that.

"Kinda sucks."

"Don't tell me that! See you tomorrow, then? Someone's calling me on the other line."

"Sure. Don't work too hard; you only have one life."

She wasn't wrong, but I wasn't either. I was trying to secure my future, making a stable platform from which I could then build a family.

Nothing wrong with that.

I dealt with the next customer and had just hung up the phone when Ritchie and Jacob returned from their trip. They came in the door and started playing a Haka in full Maori style. "Hula Waka taka maa, aloka taka maka booo," hitting their elbows and legs in their best impression of the All Blacks rugby team.

"What's up with you guys – had a magic mushroom risotto for lunch?" I asked, as soon as they'd finished the show.

"Even better. We finished a job and a nice, fat, juicy cheque is in my pocket, ready to be deposited," said Ritchie, patting his heart, or most likely the wallet inside his jacket. "And it was a success, darling. Pure love for our little firm."

Good. With success come also expenses, and now we had more mouths to feed.

"And Jacob here is a natural: I told you so."

More good news; another guy that we could now unleash and make more clients happy. Osheena also was taking new assignments, and now we really were busier than a one-legged man in a kickass contest.

"Ritchie, we also have my sister on board. She starts tomorrow."

"That's great news. Any of the bloggers?"

"I haven't reached that point yet. Would you mind looking at these few?" I said, marking their names on the list I had in front of me. "I'll take the second half."

"Sure; I'll work that out with Jacob."

I was wondering if I had to start being jealous of Jacob. He was getting all of Ritchie's attention and there was none left for me. I amused myself with the thought of just saying it out loud, but eventually thought otherwise, knowing very well that we went back a long way and had been through some difficulties.

We spent the day making calls and organising interviews for the following day. Damn, we needed my sister to take care of all these things. Every day in the office was a day in which we were not seeing customers, and competitors could have been out there eating our lunch and providing the same excellent services. We needed to hurry.

Fast, fast, fast. There was no other word in our dictionary.

CHAPTER 33

Rachel was brilliant, and not only because she was my sister; she truly was brilliant. She got the switchboard in a jiffy, and our archiving system, and she also started working straight away on a work schedule that would maximise our profits – getting the right balance on acquiring new customers, taking care of the existing ones, trips to the shops to buy stuff: the full monty.

I couldn't stay long that day, as I'd organised a dinner with Raffaele and had volunteered to do the cooking in order to apologise for not seeing him as much as I would have liked. Come on, GiGi, I said to myself: don't lie to yourself – I had to apologise for not seeing him much at all. Period.

He actually complained a couple of times and made some half-jokes about my being a ghost, or sending him a picture of myself occasionally, so that he could remember what I looked like. He was right, and I kept avoiding the issue; that was me, scooping the dirty stuff under the carpet all the time and avoiding confrontation.

The following day we were due to spend a full day doing a paintballing game with friends and I was looking forward to it, despite being a rubbish shooter. I still had my mind lost on the evening menu when Rachel came in with a letter in her hand.

"We've received an eviction notice." Calm, as if she was announcing we had some junk mail that might have been of interest.

WHAT????

"Let me see that." I snatched the letter from her hand and started reading. Yep, that was that. Eviction notice was written in bold, red letters – couldn't argue about that. I started reading and there was an awful lot of bla-bla-bla, failure to maintain the property in good repair, failure to negotiate a new lease (which was untrue; we still had two crippling years on it) and a list of other items I couldn't even comprehend. That was a mistake, for sure; but we had to do something. I looked at the leasing company name at the bottom of the letter. No phone listed. I went to the computer and started searching for Richards, Whole and Newsham, the leasing company, and there was the website. Hang on – at the very bottom it said "a Barnes Ltd Company". Could it be a company related to Jasper? I went on the Battersea Fashion Centre website and yep, there it was. A Barnes Ltd company as well. What was Jasper's problem? Why wouldn't he let it go for once?

I had to find a friend – one with a shotgun – or maybe I should start browsing one of those sites on the dark web to find a killer. I wasn't fussy; anyone who could kill would have done and I would've paid good money for that.

A plan started forming in my mind, I definitely had some dark clothes in my wardrobe; I just needed a balaclava for the newly formed GiGi Special Unit. A bunch of Ninja (actually just one, but I would recruit) ready to slip silently through the night and take revenge when the enemy was least expecting it. I imagined myself climbing walls and gutters, entering from a window accidentally left open, unsheathing my katana and … zack! A head would roll on the pavement. The next would be Lady Whilsham's and I was already seeing the headlines the day after, in bold, about the mysterious bloodshed. Poor Harry would be an orphan, but in war we can't really think too much about the innocents …

Unfortunately, my good side took over and I tried to think about options that were more reasonable.

"Rachel, could you please get Tom on the

phone?" I said. "He's listed in the system as Sloman."

"Isn't he Lillian's boyfriend? I saw him once at a dinner at your place."

"That very one, and now he's her husband."

"Cool. I liked him. I'm on it straight away."

I was fuming. I thought of sending a text to Ritchie, but it would only get him anxious and he might decide to come back to the office straight away, forgetting about his clients. A nice gesture, but we needed to keep going, no matter what.

The panic came a few minutes after, when Rachel told me Tom would look into it tomorrow. He asked if it was a court order, and apparently it wasn't (thanks to Rachel for still thinking straight), so there was no reason to worry yet.

Yeah – right. Don't worry.

I started browsing the internet, searching for a new place; I scavenged every website, but everything was so expensive. Bummer. I had the responsibility of those people working for me; Osheena had left her secure, well-paid job, and I couldn't let her down like that (or any of the others, for that matter).

Move outside London, perhaps? That could have been an option, but it would make our lives miserable. Not only would we have had to commute on a daily basis, but who would really trust a fashion consultant based in Slough? I kept browsing through the commercials, and the only things I could find in the area were warehouses –

far too expensive if you weren't selling goods. And the offices: yeah, hang on, there were some, but far too unattractive. Gosh, we just needed a decent-sized office that looked good; had they all disappeared?

Finally, I stumbled upon a good one in Lombard Street. Bingo! Just two thousand per month: that was a bargain. I had to give them a call. I looked at the agent's number and tried not to let my voice shake when I called. I soon realised, to my embarrassment, that two thousand was the price per hundred square feet; they had indeed a great office space that could be remodelled to our needs, and we could have picked up as much space as we liked.

"I have to talk to my business partner," I said at the end of that awkward conversation. Shit! I was far too naïve to live in this world. All the others that I liked were POA. I wanted to cry, go back home and hide under a duvet.

If I'd only had the capital, I could have got a major retail space, just in front of Jasper's, and shown him how things should be done! I was still shaking when, almost an hour later, I went to prepare a cup of coffee. Rachel followed me.

"Is everything OK?" she asked, pouring hot water into her cup.

"I'm just a bit nervous about the eviction, that's all," I lied. I was in full panic mode. I could accept it if I'd made a mistake, but I hadn't. Businesses close every day, owing to the economy or to bad management, and that was a risk I'd taken into account when I'd started this enterprise. What I couldn't accept was sabotage; that's what Jasper was doing, and I couldn't understand why.

"Tom said not to get worried."

"Easy for him to say, from the other end of the phone. This business is my life."

Rachel went quiet for a moment, probably pondering her position. Not a good day at the office for her; I wouldn't have blamed her if she'd decided to run at that very moment. I would have done the same.

We carried on doing our job as if nothing had happened. Eventually, at around four in the afternoon, Ritchie came back from his errands and I filled him in.

"What a bastard! I'm going to kill that little prick," he said angrily. His face was red and his fists tight; if Jasper had entered the office at that moment, he'd have been bloody murdered.

"What options do we have?" he asked eventually.

"Not many. First we have to wait for Tom's call. We faxed him the letter and he'll look into it tomorrow."

"Tomorrow's Saturday."

"He'll look into that nonetheless." I trusted him and he always delivered on his promises. That was something I was sure of: perhaps the only thing, at that very moment.

"Can we find another place in such a short

period of time?" he continued.

"I don't know. I've browsed the internet and everything seems so expensive. We're supposed to be in a recession."

"Maybe we could work from home with the existing customers. Lie low for a period of time: keep doing what we're doing until we find the right place."

We'd actually had to do that in the past, but it wasn't a good idea. We were in London; prices would never go down, and even to find this place we'd struggled and had to invest a lot of money. It would be tough.

"Perhaps," I said, not wanting Ritchie to worry. "We've been through difficult times – even worse than this. D'you remember that winter when we worked from the shed at your parents' house?"

"Oh, don't go there! It was bloody freezing, in spite of the electric heaters at full power! And that spaghetti junction we had? A single thirty-metre cable extension from the garden plug, then we had at least five power plugs connected to it – the printers, the computers, the lights, the heaters. It was a real safety hazard."

"Yeah, and when you tripped on the cable and everything came with you, crashing onto the floor … When they mention people doing things in the shed, I have a very vivid memory of what that's like."

"We were poor, but we were happy," he said, with a fake sentimental note in his voice. We both sighed, thinking of the old times, and burst out laughing. No way were we going back to that shed. Too much was at stake.

CHAPTER 34

I left the office slightly relieved; that was the effect that Ritchie had on me. No matter what, he was my rock, I could count on him to be there and pick up the pieces. I was driving towards Raffaele's place; I still had to pick up the ingredients for the dinner I was going to prepare that evening. I had a rough idea of what I would do, although I admit the kitchen is not really my domain.

The phone rang. It was my mother.

"Hello," I answered. I started hating that hands-free kit. Why was she calling now? Mothers must have some kind of radar, or some sort of hidden device that tells them when it's the least suitable moment to call. And they call nonetheless.

"Hello, sweetheart. I understand you've had a difficult day." Rachel was probably the source. We never compared notes, but I was sure Mother kept tabs on her as much as she did on me.

"Yep. Being evicted."

"It's not that easy any more, starting your own business. I remember Uncle Mick, over thirty years ago. At that time having a shop was easy: just doing the basics, paying your taxes and not much more. Nowadays, with all the laws and complications … Do you have an accountant?"

Starting my own business? Really? Where's she been for the past few years?

"Mum, what has an accountant got to do with eviction?"

"I was just saying. Keeping the books in order is important; there are so many different things that need professional advice." She kept going.

"We have Anna doing our tax and stuff."

"Yes, but she's not working there, is she? I mean, you hire her just for a month or so when you need her. It's different if you have a real employee doing these things; they'd be more trustworthy."

Anna was absolutely fine; she'd done a perfect job all these years and there had been not one single complaint from Her Majesty's Revenue and Customs; where was she going with this?

"I can't afford a full-time accountant. Not yet."

"But an employee wouldn't have overlooked such an important matter as paying the rent."

"Mother, who said I didn't pay the rent? The

money goes out every month; you know, they invented this system called a standing order." I was getting even more upset now; it wasn't enough, what I had to deal with during the day – now I also had to defend myself in front of my own mother.

"Don't be snappy, young lady. I'm just saying. So what is the issue, then?"

"I don't know what the issue is. I've asked a solicitor to look into that."

"Solicitors cost a fortune. They only care about their fees. Uncle Mick once had to go through solicitors and between their fees and what it cost going to court, he almost went bankrupt. He never fully recovered after that." GRRRRR! I started strangling the steering wheel; if someone had cut into my lane at that point, I'd have given a perfect example of road rage, one they'd remember for the rest of their life.

"I'm using Tom. He's cheap and he's a friend."

"I'd say that's a bad choice. If he's too cheap, surely he won't have the motivation to work hard enough for you? There was a friend of yours, that Christine, who went to law school – such a brilliant girl. Why didn't you call her?"

Christine who? I hadn't kept track of all my old school friends, apart from Ritchie and a few others, and I definitely didn't remember a Christine.

"I might actually do that. I think I have her number here, on my agenda," I lied.

"Well, you do that. I'll make some phone calls; we still have some family friends."

"Mother, please don't do that. Let me see what Tom has to say." When she started, it was hard to put a stop to her. The result would be that I'd have to call half of my relatives, half of her friends' friends, and spend the following week not only trying to explain the eviction but also filling them in on what I'd been doing all these years. And believe me, they would want all the details.

"I was just trying to help, but I see that it isn't appreciated."

"Mother, I really do appreciate it; it's just that I want to hear what Tom has to say first." Now she's sending me straight away through to Guilty Avenue.

"It would just be a second opinion."

"No thanks, Mother. Maybe later."

"I see you're upset now; maybe we should talk when you calm down."

"Good idea. Have a nice weekend."

"You too." She wasn't happy; I could hear it in her voice, but sometimes you have to let go. People sometimes just want to try on their own, before the cavalry gets involved.

Sainsbury's was in sight. I turned the car abruptly, causing a bit of a stir in the traffic behind me. I snatched the first parking slot I could find, and ran into the supermarket. The chances that I would be pleasant company this evening were getting slimmer by the second.

"You're early," said Raffaele as soon as I got through the door. He helped me with the groceries and followed me into the kitchen.

"I've had a rough day; I didn't want to spend one more second in there."

"Something you want to tell me?"

"Not really, apart from that we got an eviction notice." I really wasn't in the mood to repeat the whole story, especially after that phone call from Mother. It seemed that Raffaele smelled trouble.

"OK, GiGi; you let me know when you feel the time is right."

I opened a bottle and poured white wine into the biggest glass I could find. "Do you want some?" I asked, realising that I wasn't paying much attention to him.

"That would be nice." I served him a more reasonable amount, removed my jacket and started lining up the groceries.

"You sure you don't want me to cook? I really don't mind, and you seem upset."

"Not to worry. Go and relax; watch some telly and I'll call you when I'm ready." He attempted to answer back, or say something, but I was already at full speed and not in the mood for a conversation. Maybe later.

I cut the aubergine into the shape of a boat, crumbled the inside on a chopping board and cut the tomatoes. I put everything in a pan and started frying it with a bit of oil, garlic and onions. Maybe I should have done the onion first; that's what Mother would have said, but at that point I couldn't have cared less. It didn't taste of much, so

I added salt and pepper. Still not right. I rummaged in the spice cupboard and my hands stopped on the cumin. Why not? – a bit of Asian flavour. I poured a bit in the pan, mixed the lot and, for good measure, added half a glass of wine. I kept stirring until everything seemed soft enough and with a spoon I filled the aubergine boats I'd left on the side. I covered them with parmesan and tossed them into the oven. I then started preparing the risotto and, shit! I'd forgotten to buy the truffle oil. Well, you can do risotto with almost anything; it would be a variation on the theme.

More onions were chopped. I fried them first this time, put some stock on the boil and started cutting the mergueze sausages into small pieces (should I have skinned them first, maybe?). I added them to the pot to fry off and then I added the rice. As soon as I started adding the stock, I realised I'd also forgotten the saffron. Bummer.

I had to ransack Raffaele's spices again. Oregano? No, cinnamon. Maybe marjoram; no, I smelled it and didn't like it. Then I came across turmeric, rosemary and other stuff I couldn't name. Shit. Mixed spice – yes, that would do.

I threw a good amount in and for good measure threw in a bit more, and then added the wine, which should have gone in at least a couple of stages earlier; but hey, when they're in a pot they all mix together, right?

I grated some parmesan and left it on the side. That would go in at the last minute, I knew that much. I put everything on a low boil and went to Raffaele in the lounge.

"Dinner's done. We can eat when the timer goes off."

"Blimey, that was fast; if you want a job in my kitchen, just say so."

"Maybe I'll take you up on that offer."

"So, what happened today?"

I told him the full story and was grateful he didn't give advice or suggestions. I'd had too much of those for one day.

"How's the restaurant going?" I asked. The opening was approaching fast and because I was so busy with my job, coming home tired all the time, I hadn't had any time to enquire.

"I'm sorting out the menu these days. The kitchen is ready, so during the day I go there and try the new menu on the staff. We've already found the waiters and a manager to run the front. The twenty-third is just around the corner."

Shit – I'd forgotten to tell him about Natalie.

"I invited a few people for the opening. I hope you don't mind," I said sheepishly.

"Not at all. Anyone I'd know?"

"Not really." I had to tell him the full story; the more I procrastinated the worse the matter would be. "A banker from London, who might bring a customer with him. And Natalie: I told you about her. She's also bringing a friend."

"Four or five people won't be an issue. The way you were speaking, I feared you'd invited two hundred!"

I had to spill the beans. "Natalie's friend is a food critic from the *Mail*; you might have heard of her – Caroline Porter?"

"What?? You've invited a critic to the opening? Are you out of your mind?" He jumped from the sofa as if he was on springs and turned to face me, giving his best impression of a very pissed-off wolverine. "How could you do that to me? You know how much I care about that restaurant!"

"Natalie offered, and it was too late to take the invitation back," I lied. Well, I didn't lie: I just presented a slightly modified truth. "And then I thought that critics would come anyway, and you're such a good chef. Surely there would be no harm in that?"

"I don't mind critics, but not at the opening. They can make or break a business, and if she gives me a bad review, I'm finished even before I've had a chance to start." He walked up and down in the lounge like a caged tiger, trying to think what to do next, how to save the day.

"Sorry; I didn't think it would be that bad."

"The opening is pretty soon; I'll have to make everything perfect. Flipping Nora, that was a surprise."

At that moment the timer buzzed to save me from a further tirade. I left my glass on the dining table and took the aubergines out of the oven, placing them on two plates. I looked at the risotto and it appeared on the dry side, so I added more stock.

"Et voilà: my interpretation of jambalaya."

We sat at the table and as soon as Raffaele tasted the aubergine, I knew something had gone deeply wrong. He almost choked, but out of respect he swallowed the bite. Maybe that was just his way of demonstrating he was upset; it couldn't possibly be that bad. I tasted mine and it wasn't bad at all. It was DISGUSTING!

"How many times you have prepared this dish before?" he asked, as if he was John Torode judging one of the Masterchef contestants, possibly a less talented one.

"Well, with these very ingredients, this is the first time."

"So you decided to cook, and you prepared something you've never done before?"

"I thought it would test my creativity."

"Yes, and my taste buds. You could start a career in the rat-poisoning industry if you carry on like that," he laughed. I laughed as well: it was that bad. Or, it could be a new dieting craze! Cook something that tastes so disgusting that people just can't eat it. So, by making them completely lose their appetite, they lose weight! He looked set to come out with more along the same lines, so I quickly said, "Mind if we skip to the main course?" I took his plate, not giving him a chance for further criticism.

"What's next?" A worried look was painted on his face.

"I've made a risotto; you can't go wrong with that."

"I'll be the judge of that."

The main course was no better than the starter. I tried it first, to avoid being influenced by such a severe judge, but the dish was a total disaster. If I'd wanted to cook something horrible on purpose, I couldn't have achieved a better result. I tried to stop Raffaele, but it was too late; the fork was already in his mouth. He spat out the lot, screaming

"What the hell? What did you actually put in this concoction of yours? I can't even recognise the flavours."

"It's a simple risotto; I don't understand. I just added some spices."

"Which ones?" he asked, inquisitively. He was now in full Hercule Poirot mode, trying to find the murder weapon.

"I just added some mixed herbs," I said innocently.

"There are no mixed herbs in here. Show me."

I went to the kitchen, found the jar and brought it back to the table "Here, see for yourself."

"GiGi, that is mixed spice, used for cakes, not for savoury dishes."

"Oh!"

We looked at each other and started laughing. "I take back my offer to employ you in my kitchen."

"I don't blame you." Shit, I had completely ruined dinner. "What now?"

"We can order a pizza if you like."

"Yes please. A pepperoni one for me." I excused myself and went to the bathroom. The surprises weren't finished for the day yet: I'd just found out I had my period.

CHAPTER 35

"Any news from Tom?" asked Ritchie as soon as I entered the room.

"He thinks it's all bullshit and they have no grounds to evict us, but we might have to go to court if they insist." I hung up my jacket, tossed my bag onto a chair nearby and went straight over to the coffee machine. Once I had a hot cup in my hands, the world appeared less grim than it had been; it always worked. I sat on a chair nearby and started sipping.

"How was the weekend?" he asked

"Paintball tournament with Raffaele, Tom and Lillian and another couple. Apparently I got a new nickname: Xena."

"Like the warrior princess in the series. It suits you." He was still looking at the computer and I could see some interesting items. He was browsing a shoe manufacturer in Italy – shoes that sold at six hundred pounds a pair. Wow.

"Yeah, I was so upset I almost killed everybody. What did they say? – that I was trigger-happy. What about yours?"

"Jonathan and I went to see 'La Bohème' on Saturday. We'd never been to the opera before and thought of giving it a try."

I wasn't passionate about that kind of music. There had been a period when I was stuck in the eighties, because that was what my parents had listened to, and then I went straight into the new century.

"Was it good?"

"Oh, darling, I've never cried so much in my life! The beginning is very cheerful, and they give you this book with the translation and all, so you can follow what they're singing. So you're always reading, looking, and reading. When Mimi died at the end, I was in full Bublé mode, 'Cry me a River'."

"Sounds fun." Ritchie was always able to surprise me, coming out with something totally different all the time. Once he had a wristwatch period and studied every possible brand that was out there. Then he had the Japanese literature period. Every week he had a different book – Mishima, Tanizaki, you name it – and then the

South American period started: literature, Brazilian music and so on. I guess that was his personal way of developing: picking random things, becoming almost an expert, and then moving on to something new. Probably that was the secret of how he always got along well with everybody. No matter what your interest was, Richie had been there and read something about it.

"Oh it was, darling, believe me. And then we had a night at the Dorchester."

"A what?"

"Well, we thought it would be nice having dinner and something to drink before the opera, and not be in a mad rush to go home. So we booked a night at the Dorchester, just to pamper ourselves a bit. We are working our socks off, you know."

I knew exactly what he was saying; we spent hours and hours every day working hard and we needed some quality time with our partners. I thought I would nick the Dorchester idea for Raffaele.

"And then Sunday morning," he continued, "we went wandering in Camden Market and had some street food. We went home at six-ish, but it was a good break. I feel energised."

I told him about my disastrous dinner on Friday night, and fortunately he didn't rub salt in my wounds. He'd experienced some of my cooking; something he was still probably trying to forget. We went quiet for a moment, and then Ritchie asked, "So what do we do?", obviously referring to the eviction notice.

"We carry on as if nothing is happening. Tom says not to worry and I trust him. If indeed we have to spend money on going to court, well, that's the right motivation to bring in even more business."

"Hmm: risky." Ritchie wasn't fully convinced. Fortunately, Osheena and Jacob also came in at that time, so I filled them in about the eviction and the plan to go full steam ahead. They were enthusiastic.

Osheena in particular was pushing on the website where our office was and she had decided to have "visiting times", like when you go to the doctor. Make an appointment, come to us and we'll assess your needs and give you direction. It was a risky move, because people would have to pass phase one alone, admitting they had a wardrobe problem; but my doubts vanished a few minutes later.

"You won't believe it," she said showing me her phone. "During the weekend we got at least a hundred emails asking for an appointment here at the office. OK, they're all Advanced offerings, so we won't make a huge amount of money, but still – a hundred customers coming through the door … If we do our job right, we could go viral."

Oh, the power of the internet. I was barely in my thirties and already felt like a dinosaur, considering how fast things were moving online compared to my old-fashioned approach. But I guess there might be some talent in having the ability to surround yourself with people that will help you grow. I had something there: the ability of giving the right people a chance, and if I'd made mistakes in the past, it was true that I was now in the black and people worked hard for that single opportunity I gave them. It made me proud. They made me proud.

We decided that Ritchie and Jacob would go out and continue their job with the Platinum customers (and they loved it anyway), while Osheena and I would take care of the office and the "visitors". I quickly checked my emails and got an even bigger surprise: at least twenty bloggers were ready to collaborate with us. A few of them even thought they could bring in their followers, as a portfolio of customers.

That was a biggie, so I called all the guys into the meeting room before they disappeared on the road. Ritchie and I usually had the final word on how to manage the business; however, we'd grown accustomed to trusting our two new companions, to the point where they were allowed to make their own decisions in their respective sectors. Osheena, in particular, was a machine. She had more ideas than she could even put into practice and, because of her work alone, the business was thriving and a wider audience had become aware of us. I would remember that at bonus time.

"So, guys, here are the facts. We've got some

followers and potential partners coming our way. D'you remember we got in touch with the bloggers?"

A unanimous chorus of "yes" followed.

"Well, we have at least twenty of them interested in collaborating. How are we going to play this one?"

Ritchie was the first to speak "Let's assume we're picky and we agree to work only with the best, let's say five or six. Each one of them has thousands of followers. We have to balance it right."

"You're right," interjected Jacob. "Get too many and we wouldn't be able to cope. That would be a huge dissatisfaction to our clients and could turn them against us."

"And these people are trendsetters, good at spotting what's new and cool, but we need to ensure that our customers come first. We don't want our customers wearing something that doesn't suit them, or doesn't make them happy, just because it's trendy. This has been the core business of this firm; we aren't going to alienate it," I said, in a very … business-like tone. Oh GiGi: don't transform yourself into a corporate monster, I thought; you know you hate that sort of thing.

Osheena was the first to build on the idea. "Business units," she said, without even looking up from the block notes she was scribbling on.

We looked at each other as if she was speaking a different language. She smiled, took her time in savouring the moment, as all of our tongues were hanging out waiting for her next words. Finally she said, "Business units. We can have many of them; each consultant has their own, and each one has its own style. Contemporary, high fashion and so on."

"Maybe it's because it's Monday and I've had a rough weekend," said Jacob, "but I don't get it!"

"Think about it," continued Osheena, who by then was on a roll. "We get one of these bloggers – take this Trendygirl, for example." She turned her laptop so we could take a good look at her blog. "She's for trendy casual, so every customer who would fit in that category would go to her. And it's scalable; if she has too many customers, all of us can give her a hand or, in the future, we could hire people to work in her department; people that are in sync with her style. And so on with all the others."

"Sounds like a franchise," said Ritchie, mulling the matter over. Good: I wasn't the only one taking that suggestion seriously.

"Each blogger has their own division," I repeated, "It's just brilliant. They wouldn't have to give up their ideas or their talent; they'd have a platform to put it into practice and earn. Am I the only one thinking that this could really be the next big thing in town?"

They were looking at each other, nodding and smiling; it was evident we agreed on what was the best direction we should all follow. The next discussion expanded on Osheena's idea; we evaluated the pros and the cons, but we couldn't really find any reason why it shouldn't work. It was easy; everybody could make money and nobody would lose independence or limit their own creativity. This was exactly why Osheena had been so frustrated in her previous job. It was brilliant.

The meeting was over, but Ritchie stayed behind. When the door was closed he said, "We're lucky to have them."

I agreed with him wholeheartedly. "We're getting better and better."

"I was thinking: they really are putting their heart and soul into this for us," he continued, almost embarrassed. They were doing a great job, there was no question – so what was this all about?

"OK, spit it out. What d'you have in mind?"

"I was thinking that, maybe, they should become partners in our firm. Look at what Osheena did with the online part. And Jacob: well, customers just love him. He's bringing in new customers all the time; he seems to know half of London."

As usual, Ritchie was ahead of me. I was thinking in terms of bonuses, while he was already thinking about partnerships. These two exceptional people would have the right motivation if they were fighting for their own business: not that they hadn't already shown their worth – far from it. They were putting in as many hours as Ritchie and me, and eventually they could run out of steam if they were just employees.

As I went quiet, pondering the idea and loving it at the same time, Ritchie interpreted my silence as disagreement.

"Look, GiGi, they don't have to be equal partners, but they deserve something. We are making pots of money and …"

"Hold on; you don't have to convince me. OK, they become partners. You figure out the details, and I'm sure you'll do it fairly."

"Thank you, GiGi. You won't regret it …"

I interrupted him. "And you'll also have to tell them. It's your idea, after all." I grinned like a Cheshire cat when saying that. I knew him far too well and that he'd love being the one to tell them. It was his idea after all; he should get the credit.

What a journey we'd had so far. From the very beginning, scraping by, then a potential disaster, to my almost losing Ritchie as a friend in the process, and then to have bounced back to where we were now…

"OK, now go and visit your clients, I have a packed morning with bloggers and customers."

He picked up his laptop and ran towards Jacob, who was already waiting impatiently by the door.

CHAPTER 36

During the following couple of weeks we interviewed all the bloggers. We devised a simple mechanism; Osheena would do the first pass and write down her own notes, then I did the same. At the end of the day, we would meet and put on a write-and-wipe board our preferences, what struck us most about each candidate, whether we thought they'd fit with the team and so on. Some of them were keen on keeping their own independence, and I actually loved that idea, while others just wanted a job. We needed some entrepreneurial initiative in our firm, and therefore we discarded the latter group. We also had a good list of candidates for the "regular" jobs as consultants: it's all well and good having people with ideas, but if you don't have enough of a workforce to take care of the customers, you go out of business.

Things were taking shape, and with Osheena's input we were working like a well-oiled machine. We also fitted in time for all the Advanced customers who wrote to us – hundreds of them. A few were disappointed about the long waiting list, but most just accepted it as part of the experience of having a fashion consultant on their side. We already had a couple of people ready to come in and give us a hand and they were completing their training during that time. When I say "training" I have to clarify: you can't really train someone in our job. We had to spot the right person, who had to demonstrate personality, clear ideas on fashion and a love for what we were doing. The training was to ensure they understood our mentality; how we operated with our clients and what made us special. Failure to adhere to our strict rules would mean customer dissatisfaction – not that this had happened previously, but I was keen to explain it upfront.

So, on the one side I had a thriving business, and on the other side my love life had started, yet again, to look more and more like a disaster zone. Raffaele was brilliant with me; that very weekend we had the restaurant opening and during this whole period he had demonstrated to me, on many occasions, how supportive he was. However, we'd started arguing more often, sometimes over something silly like what we were watching on TV, or what I wanted for dinner. That had happened the previous morning; I was late for work and he had asked me what I would prefer in the evening: salmon en croute or quails. For me, everything he was cooking was delicious, so I said it didn't really matter.

Well, never tell a chef that it doesn't matter what he cooks; he'll take it personally. He went on a rampage about leaving everything up to him, from cooking to sorting out the house, to the fact that in the evening I was always tired (he actually used the zombie word) and that we had little time for ourselves. It almost sounded as though we weren't a couple any more.

I found that extremely annoying, and I let him know in clear terms. We were building our own spaces in the world, him with the restaurant and me … well, things had never been better. I was young and I needed to fulfil my dream, to see this business going through and become an established one. We would have time to relax later, in the future.

Unfortunately, he didn't receive that speech very well, which fuelled another discussion. We left each other bitterly that morning, and the following evening we barely spoke.

I looked at the balance sheet on the computer and it looked very good. We were wealthy; the cash flow was brilliant and we could even have afforded a few rainy days (actually a whole monsoon period) without bringing us to our knees. I left the office at four and drove to the restaurant, where I hoped things would have settled down with Raffaele.

Guests were due to arrive at half past six, to have a few drinks, listen to the speech and dinner would start at half past seven. For those not willing to drive back, there were rooms above the restaurant. I'd actually had Ritchie looking into that, so that every room would look amazing. That had caused additional friction between Raffaele and me, but, he eventually accepted Ritchie's ideas.

Raffaele was at full steam ahead in the kitchen, so I just said "hello" through the door. Tom and Lillian arrived a few minutes later, followed by Timothy, his wife and a friend and, by a quarter to seven, the whole restaurant was already packed.

The waiters were friendly; people snatched at the nibbles in a matter of seconds and seemed to be enjoying the jovial atmosphere in the restaurant: it was a perfect evening. Eventually Natalie arrived, just a few minutes after seven, with her friend from the *Mail*.

"Hello." I kissed her and shook hands with the journalist, Caroline Porter. "I'm really glad you could make it."

"Oh darling, I wouldn't have missed this for anything in the world!"

"Nice place you guys have here. Very friendly," said Caroline.

"Maybe I should introduce you to the chef?" I

asked her. I saw Raffaele had just finished his speech and that it would be the perfect occasion to show there was nothing to be worried about.

"No need, my dear. I prefer that it's the food speaking to me."

Oh shit – maybe Raffaele had been right after all.

A waiter approached us and brought our two guests to their table. I'd have time to catch up with Natalie later, after the dessert. The place was really buzzing and people were enjoying themselves. It was a happy place and I really hoped that Caroline Porter wasn't about to kill my boyfriend's dream on that very first opening night.

I sat at a small table in the bar area and had a little plate of carpaccio and a beer while everybody else was busy, the customers eating and the staff serving. I'd received plenty of emails and while Raffaele was busy, I tried to catch up with work.

Suddenly a familiar voice echoed through the bar, not too far away from where I was sitting. "We've waited a full ten minutes for our drinks. Where's our champagne?"

I looked in disbelief at Jasper relieving his frustration against the poor waiter, who promptly answered, "I'll see what I can do, sir, I'll look into the matter myself."

"That's not good enough, boy," he continued, "You should have thought about that when there was time. What kind of circus are you running here? Don't you care about paying customers?"

He was looking around, trying to catch signs of approval from nearby guests, when our eyes locked. If people were watching, they'd be hard put to decide which of us was looking at the other with more hatred. He let go of the waiter and approached my table.

"Well, well, GiGi Griswald. Apparently they're letting everybody into these premises."

"Sure they are, if you're here," I retorted. How in hell he'd managed to get onto the guest list was a mystery I hadn't solved yet. I certainly hadn't seen his name anywhere; was he perhaps crashing the party, just for the sake of it? "What are you doing here anyway?"

"I've been invited, of course. A rich developer from London had the invitation and he thought of extending it to me. I bet that little business of yours has finally failed. Are you working here now?"

He was a nasty little man, although not in the literal sense (he was quite tall as it happened); how in hell had I got involved with him in the first place? "No, I'm not working here; I happen to know the guy who owns the place."

"Not for long, if he keeps treating his customers like this. The service is appalling."

"No, it isn't. They're probably used to dealing with much more civilised people rather than bullies."

His face turned red and he raised his voice. "How dare you call me a bully? I'm a paying customer, and I deserve to be properly hosted." A few people from the main dining area started turning their heads. After a few seconds, Lady PlumInHerMouth also came to join her former husband. Clearly, we were interrupting some business matter.

"I don't mean to be rude, but where is our champagne?" Oh dear, she was repeating Jasper's words; makes you wonder why they divorced in the first place. I was almost ready to give up and go back to my little table – after all, I was a guest the same as everybody else – when Raffaele came out of the kitchen.

"What seems to be the problem?" he asked, seeing the three of us, plus the waiter, standing in front of the bar.

"The problem is, young man," Jasper said, "that you don't know the basic principles of running a restaurant. Have you ever heard of the sentence 'Customers come first'?"

Now, that was a cheap shot. This had nothing to do with Raffaele and his restaurant; Jasper was just being mean.

"I ask again: what's the problem?" This time Raffaele's tone of voice was firm and upset.

"We've been waiting for ages for our champagne. Did you send someone to France to get it or something?"

Raffaele turned towards the waiter as if to ask for an explanation, and the guy said, "The beverages are at the table, sir. It's that one in the corner. The waiter asked the other guest, as he was alone, if he wanted it served, but the guest said to come back in a few minutes once his two visitors had returned to the table."

"You little liar! How dare you? We left the table for just a few minutes."

"Please wait here." Raffaele went into the main dining room and chatted for a few minutes with the guest in question, who was still sitting at his table. They seemed to be friendly, as if they had known each other for ages. Raffaele returned and, with a grin on his face, said, "You are not welcome in my restaurant. I'd like you to leave."

"That is unacceptable …" Lady Whilsham started, but Raffaele stopped her mid-sentence.

"You can either leave or I can have you thrown out. Your choice." His tone of voice left no room for negotiation and a couple of waiters came around, bringing the couple's coats.

"That is outrageous," said Jasper. "I've never been treated like this before in my entire life. I will ruin you – I know influential people … And you …" – pointing his finger right in my face – "I'll see you in court!"

Raffaele went back to the kitchen without saying a word as soon as they left, while some of the waiters and guests started giggling to themselves at the scene. I went back to my table to try to catch up with my work. What an idiot that Jasper is.

Time flies when you're busy and I hadn't noticed when the first guests started leaving. It was only when Timothy and his wife approached me that I realised it was almost ten in the evening.

"I hope you've enjoyed your dinner," I said

"Everything was fabulous, my dear. This boyfriend of yours deserves a Michelin star, straight away."

"I've been in many restaurants," added the banker's guest, whose name I didn't catch, "but this surpassed them all. I will definitely be bringing my own clients here for a treat." We spent a few more minutes exchanging pleasantries, then Timothy and company left the building. That was a relief, I knew Raffaele was a great chef, but my opinion was biased, wasn't it?

Natalie was still around. They had both decided to stay for the night and Caroline Porter had already left for her room. Natalie explained that she was in her late sixties, full of energy when it was a matter of food, but easily tired after an evening out.

"So, what do you think? Did she like it?"

"Well, I loved it, but Caroline isn't letting the cat out of the bag. She's always been like that, and I know better than to ask, especially if I've been invited to a friend's restaurant. I guess we'll find out next week, in her column."

Bummer: a secretive critic, exactly what I needed. Now I had to wait almost a full week before even knowing if she liked the opening or not. That was unnerving, especially with the tension already existing between Raffaele and me.

We shared a beer at the bar; I told her about how

the business was growing and she responded by talking about her new boyfriend. She was happy, but I was not.

CHAPTER 37

I went to bed at around eleven that night and Raffaele reached me much later, at around one if I remember correctly. I heard him tossing and turning, but hardly a word passed between us. I could only imagine how stressful the evening had been, being the opening night and all, but, Raffaele said nothing to me. At some point he turned towards me and at least gave me a cuddle, which at that time was as much as I needed, as I was still frantic about what review Caroline Porter might write about the restaurant. I'd been doing my own share of tossing and turning before Raffaele had come to bed – about the business, the restaurant, our relationship and so on. I fell into a fitful sleep and the last thing I remember was hoping, against all hope, that she didn't trash the food, the atmosphere, the service, or anything else for that matter.

I didn't wake up in time for breakfast or, at least, I had a lie-in. Raffaele probably sneaked out very early to assist in the kitchen. Blimey, it was already eleven in the morning and, for sure, Natalie and Caroline Porter had already left.

I had a warm shower, but that didn't wake me up completely either. With the restaurant officially open, a few people had started coming through the door by the time I went downstairs. I popped into the kitchen and said a quick hello to Raffaele, who was busy preparing for the lunch service. I thought about taking one of the bicycles that we had in the shed, but the weather wasn't promising and I still had a lot of work to take care of, so I drove home.

It was comforting receiving a few messages of thanks, including from Timothy and Natalie, but to be honest the dangling sword of Caroline Porter was the one that worried me. What a disaster it would be if she said something negative! I spent the afternoon working on the bloggers' files; we had some decisions to make the following Monday and I wanted to be fully prepared.

Raffaele came home very late and we barely spoke; he was still fuming about our discussion earlier. If I'd had the power to turn the clock back, I would have done it immediately. I knew my nature was impulsive, but I had to do better, much better, if I wanted to succeed both in my private life and in my career.

The week went by uneventfully, and that included my private life. We were giving the final push to get the bloggers on board and I worked until late at night every single day. Maybe it was an excuse to avoid another confrontation with Raffaele and although he was more relaxed about it (he said that, eventually, food critics would have made an appearance anyway), I still felt guilty. There was nothing I could do about it; that was me, but even if he wasn't upset any more I couldn't stop beating myself up about it. I kept thinking about how I could have managed things differently, what I should have said.

The good news came towards the end of the week, and it was Tom himself bringing it to us. "We won!" he shouted, coming into the office and fluttering a piece of paper in the air as if it was a victory flag.

We all knew what he was talking about: the elephant in the room that nobody had dared to mention during all this time – the litigation against Barnes concerning these premises. The fact was that Jasper had also tried to evict all the other tenants in the building. Tom researched it and found out that half of the offices were empty – surely Jasper's doing – but all the remaining ones were as upset as we were.

We looked at each other in disbelief when Tom

fell silent: a lawyer's trick, for sure, to create more drama.

"Come on, Tom! Don't leave us hanging here," shouted Ritchie, who was already on his feet and ready to grab the paper from him.

"Guys, let's go into the meeting room; this is something everybody needs to hear," I said. We went into the boardroom (we called it that, but in reality it was a meeting room just slightly bigger than the other two), and for once I felt as if we were a proper business. I looked at Osheena, Ritchie, Jacob and the two bloggers who had started that very week. Indeed, it looked like a proper team, a real firm, by now.

"Tom, please go ahead; we're all in trepidation to hear the news."

"Well, as you know, I visited all the other tenants in this building." Oh dear, he was going for the long version. That would be worse than awaiting the results of the *X Factor*: a lot of pauses and tricks to keep us hanging on every single word he was going to say.

"I soon found out that they'd all received the same letter you had," he continued. We all nodded. "Believe me, some of the guys were really upset, but I managed to get them on board, one by one. Once I explained that we needed to fight united, half the job was done." He was putting a lot of emphasis into his speech. I guess everybody deserves their own Braveheart moment in life.

"I'll save you all the effort I had to put in, in

analysing the contracts, tenancy agreements, letters and emails. Believe me, it was hard work, but someone had to do it." People would have laughed (had they known him) at his attempt to be serious. "The judge was implacable and for a moment we thought everything was lost. It was only after a strenuous battle and my willingness to face peril that eventually justice prevailed."

Ritchie intervened: "By losing, you could have started a new career as a comedian." Everybody laughed, but Tom kept his poker face on and continued undaunted. "At the very last minute, we were able to swing the judgment in our favour. We found the smoking gun, that very piece of evidence that every detective dreams about coming across and, by presenting it, the judge (who was surely in Barnes' pocket) couldn't deny us justice." And so, he rested his case, as if we were his jury, and recited his closing statement.

We looked at each other in disbelief, when finally Osheena asked the question that everybody in the room was thinking that very same moment, "Which was?"

Tom took a deep breath, like a teacher annoyed by having to explain every single detail to his pupils, and answered, "Barnes had planning permission to demolish this building and erect instead a set of new condos, the expensive kind. Once I'd made clear to the judge that the real reason behind the eviction was pure greed, his hands were tied. He had to agree with us," he said in a grave voice, shaking his head and nodding to his little audience, as if to celebrate the victory of justice against felony.

We all sighed with relief and after congratulating Tom for his heroic effort, saving all of us from despair, there was only one remaining question to ask.

"Was Jasper in court?" asked Ritchie.

"He was indeed, and so was his ex-wife. If looks could kill, I wouldn't like to be their poor lawyer. He was quiet in court, but as soon as they exited, the shouting and screaming started. Blimey, he was livid. His face was completely red when he was shouting and for a moment I thought he was going to have a heart attack."

People were cheering about the unexpected victory and as soon as I had captured Ritchie's attention I gave him a sign. It was time.

He put his feet down and repeatedly hit a glass with his pen, in order to capture the audience's attention. "Ladies and Gentlemen," he started, "today we celebrate the victory against the empire of evil, but the good news hasn't ended." People started looking at each other, expecting some kind of joke, which wouldn't have been completely strange coming from Ritchie.

"As a firm we're doing great. Well, you know very well we are, but I assure you there have been times when GiGi and I have scratched our heads and seriously thought we would be better off on a remote island taking care of a flock of sheep. That is no longer the case."

Come on, get to the point, I thought, and looking at the other's faces they were probably thinking the same.

"The first piece of good news is that, for this year, we will all enjoy a healthy bonus." Cheers erupted. "We haven't worked out the figures yet, but we'll be as generous as we can."

Cheers erupted in the room again. We were new to the business – having to deal with other people, that is – as it had always been Ritchie and me for all those years. We were learning quickly that, by working as a team, we would be even more successful. All of them were working hard to make this firm successful; they deserved to be recognised.

"The second bit of good news is that Osheena and Jacob have been promoted to partners, effective immediately."

For a moment, the room fell silent as that information started to sink in. Then they both dropped their jaws in surprise. They were looking at each other, as if to confirm that they'd heard correctly. The first one to speak was Jacob and in a squeaky, trembling voice, he asked, "Are you kidding us? You mean, partners partners?"

Everyone laughed at their surprise and suddenly people started clapping their hands. Jacob became red-faced, like a little pupil caught in an embarrassing situation.

"But …why?" Osheena asked then.

"Well, in your case because of all your work on the internet – setting up the website, the blog, getting the bloggers working with us, in addition to taking care of your clients," answered Ritchie "And more, which at the moment I forget. Trust me, you deserve it. You already work as if you're an integral part of this firm, not as a simple employee, and both GiGi and I recognise that. And you, Jacob: your brilliant job with our top customers. You almost bring in more revenue than anyone else, and the clients all adore you. I can't think about this firm without you any more. We had to do something."

Osheena was crying; she'd been stuck in a job that she hated when we met and now she was in control of her own destiny. We had given her the chance of shaping her new work and she'd done it brilliantly.

"How can I ever thank you?" She started sobbing, but Ritchie was already by her side and gave her a comforting hug. If someone had asked why I was getting up in the morning and doing what I do, I would have answered, "To get the chance of seeing days like this."

The meeting was soon over and everybody went back to their work in good spirits.

CHAPTER 38

Jasper was out of the equation (or so I thought), but his presence remained between Raffaele and me. We had our final row a few days afterwards, when probably we said way too many things; things that we would possibly regret in the future.

His main point, to my surprise, was not about Jasper or Caroline Porter. "You work too much; we barely see each other," he said.

"I know that, but for once we're being really successful. We have lots to do; we're thinking about expanding further ..."

"When will it be enough? How big does your firm have to be, before you slow down?"

I admit I hadn't thought about that. For me, it

was my creation, something that Ritchie and I had built, and frankly we'd never thought deeply about where we'd want to stop. If ever. Don't they say that in *Dragon's Den*? To be successful, a business also has to be scalable. Who knows what the future had lined up for me? Maybe my own brand of designer clothes, or perhaps a perfume. Who knows?

"I don't know when I want to stop – I mean, not yet; there's so much to do." I tried to justify myself. But maybe I shouldn't have; after all, it was my own life we were talking about. "You have your own business too; you know it takes effort to make it work."

"GiGi, I'm not working harder than any other chef. On the contrary, I've found a very capable sous-chef, who can cover for me whenever I want. Life is there to be enjoyed. Sure, we have to work, but it shouldn't be instead of having a private life. I sorted out things in such a way that I could be free to spend time with you. What have you done on that front?"

I was furious. How dare he ask me to renounce my job? Technically, he hadn't asked that; he'd asked me to slow down, which was somewhat fair, but that wasn't the point. The point was that … Well, I had to admit that I didn't know yet what the point was, but that wasn't the point either. I was trying to build for our future, to have something that was really mine.

We went on for hours and eventually we

decided that it was better to take a break from each other; maybe the distance would help to clear our minds a bit more. To be honest it wasn't exactly a joint decision; it was more me saying I had to think stuff over and see how I settled. He was more on the "Let's try to figure out something together" idea, but honestly, I couldn't see how I could have slowed down right at that moment, with all the success I was having. Eventually I packed my stuff (fortunately, most of my clothes were still at my place) and left.

I was right.

I was a hundred per cent sure I was right.

So, what was that feeling, all that sadness, that engulfed me while I was driving home? I could barely see the road, I was shattered, in tears and crying like a baby. I reached home and looked at the empty fridge and soon realised how much I loved Raffaele, how we enjoyed our dinners. Even the one I'd prepared was a funny moment, although it had been inedible. I missed our time together already – our laughter, the simple moments spent on the sofa cuddling each other.

Gosh, how I cried that night!

Jasper came to visit us the following day and that was indeed unexpected.

Jonathan, Ritchie's boyfriend, had turned up at the office to take him out for lunch and was just saying, "What a lovely office you have here," when Jasper popped in.

We were all by the main entrance exchanging greetings and we saw Ritchie sprinting as if he was Usain Bolt; he narrowly avoided Jonathan by a bare inch by twisting his body, and before we could even say "Dolce and Gabbana" he had smashed his fist into Jasper's nose.

I'm not a violent type, but hey, it was like watching Mike Tyson at his best. Shame he didn't bite his ears off.

Jasper fell to the ground like a dropped sack of potatoes and thank God that with Jonathan's reflexes the boxing match didn't turn into a cage fight. My money would have been on Ritchie, anyway.

"YOU BASTARD! HOW DARE YOU SHOW YOUR FACE IN HERE …?" Ritchie was shouting, while his partner tried to keep him away from Jasper, who was now sitting by the door with a handkerchief in his hand, trying to stop the bleeding.

"Jonathan, take him to the other room. Please," I wasn't happy to have him removed from the hall, but I also wanted to avoid him having a criminal record.

"What are you doing here, Jasper?" I asked, while he was getting up. Good. Not too much damage done – or maybe it was bad: I still hadn't made my mind up.

"I come in peace; I have an offer to make," he finally said, cleaning his nose and sorting out his jacket.

"What d'you mean, an offer? I've heard enough of that from you in the past and you should know what my answer is," I retorted. I was ready to punch him myself.

"It's a different one, this time. Is there somewhere we could talk?"

I accompanied him to the boardroom and then went to get Osheena and Jacob, the new partners and, if he had calmed down enough, even Ritchie.

"I don't mind hearing what the slippery snake has to say," Ritchie said. Jonathan had managed to temper his rage but obviously he was still red in the face. "Whatever he says, it's going to be a lie."

"Sure; but we can always say 'no', and to be honest I'm not inclined to listen to him either. But let's just see what he wants," I said.

We went back in the boardroom where our other two partners were already waiting. They were fuming; I could see the belligerent look on their faces. I sat opposite Jasper and kept Ritchie on my right, ready to stop him if he looked as if he was going to punch our unwanted guest again.

"OK, Jasper; have your say."

He looked around and said "All four of you? I don't think what I have to say is for the staff to hear."

If he didn't choose his words carefully, he'd be at the receiving end of Osheena's and Jacob's punches this time, and possibly mine too.

"It's not your concern who's listening or who isn't. I repeat, say what you have to say," I said; my voice was almost trembling. I was upset, and struggling not to give him a tongue-lashing.

"Very well; you manage your firm the way you like," he said, showing his disapproval of the situation. "The reality is that even if you've won in court, I can still throw you out of this building in a couple of years' time; we have a clause for that."

Gee, he was arrogant; how in hell had I thought at some point that he was attractive? I must have been drunk.

He continued, "I'm prepared to make you an offer, but it'll be valid only for a few days. Consider it carefully, because there won't be another one." He paused and looked at each one of us as if to make his point clear. "I can offer you fifty thousand pounds if you leave next month. Cash. Where you go is none of my business, and the offer isn't negotiable. Think about it."

Ritchie was the first to answer, "I'll tell you what you can do with your offer: you can shove it up …"

"Ritchie!" I said, stopping him mid-sentence and putting my hand on his arm – both to emphasise he shouldn't get himself into more trouble and also to have a firm grip on him in case he tried to assault Jasper again.

To my surprise, and before I could say anything, both Osheena and Jacob intervened. "You can forget about that," she said, which was followed by Jacob's "No way."

Jasper tried to add, "It isn't your call to …" but I

stopped him mid-sentence.

"Hold your horses, cowboy. Everybody here has a say, and you'd better start listening."

Ritchie regained control of himself, looked at me and, when I smiled at him, he said, "Well, I think the majority of this firm has taken a decision. Which is – we reject your offer, just to make it clear."

Jasper's face was red with anger and no doubt frustration; he was attempting to say something else when Jacob intervened. "This meeting is over. You can either walk out now or we can accompany you." He then grinned at Ritchie, who was ready for a second round.

The message was received by Jasper, who stood up and left the room. As soon as he closed the door, a chorus of "Hurrah!" exploded in the room.

Someone even showed fingers at the door.

CHAPTER 39

Caroline Porter's review was in the paper; Rachel showed it to me that morning. I took the paper, but avoided reading it until I had my coffee ready and was within the safety of my office.

I sat at my desk and opened the Mail.

New Restaurant Review by Caroline Porter

Today I want to tell you about a new restaurant in Surrey: The Skittish Endeavours Gastro Pub.

Some of you living around Warlingham might remember the old name, the White Horse. Well, forget about that; the restaurant is now in a very different league and nothing to do with the old trough.

Having been fully refurbished, yet still maintaining its old-world charm, the building itself has remained relatively unchanged. However, from the first look at the menu to the last bite of my dessert, I have to admit that I was thoroughly impressed. The food, I hate to say it, was "to die for" and that is not a phrase I use lightly. The atmosphere and service were impeccable.

The young chef is an Italian/American called Raffaele Nesti, who has worked with some of the most influential Michelin-starred chefs in both this country and abroad. If this might put some of you off, don't let it. He is not one of those chefs using the sous vide method to cook their salmon, making it an inedible mushy, slimy mess. Or worse, one of those chefs so full of themselves that they tend to forget what is important – taste – and put pesto over your pannacotta. You surely remember my review last month of that Mayfair restaurant, so promising on paper ...

No – Raffaele, as I said, is in a different league; flavour is what really matters, accompanied by beautiful presentation. I had an excellent starter of chicken liver terrine with bone marrow and truffle to die for. Have you ever kissed a plate in your life? I ate my starter and then snogged the plate, leaving it completely clean.

The main course was a saffron risotto accompanied by oxtail, surely braised in beautiful flavours of celery, carrots, sage, thyme, tomato and spices for hours and hours: Italian passion transformed into a dish. If you ever wanted to have an affair, have it with one of Raffaele Nesti's main courses. They will seduce you, make you sweat with desire, take you to (gastronomic) places you could never have imagined or even for that matter known existed and, most of all from an Italian food lover, they will leave you completely satisfied.

I finished with a hazelnut soufflé that would have revived Escoffier himself and made him livid and ashamed. A soufflé light as a feather, tall and aroused, sorry, raised like the Gherkin Tower and ready to fulfil all the promises your senses were waiting for. A delicious ice cream, which I cannot even start to describe, accompanied the soufflé: you will just have to taste it for yourself.

Every single plate was as beautiful as a picture, but we are not talking here about a Picasso or a Mondrian. Here we are in the Caravaggio territory, the Rembrandt, vibrant with colours but with the addition of other dimensions.

Whether you want a romantic meal for two in a quiet little corner or need the room for a family gathering, this place has it all.

And if you're going to visit the restaurant with your partner, the venue offers accommodation at a reasonable price above the restaurant. You will need it, after your senses have been shaken from head to toe eating all those fantastic masterpieces.

It is rare to find such a gem of a restaurant, especially as this is chef Raffaele's first solo venture. I would thoroughly recommend The Skittish Endeavour Gastro Pub, no matter what your taste in food, as I'm sure you will find something to suit you on their small but very well-formed menu.

Caroline Porter

I was astounded by what I had just read. I knew Caroline Porter from having read a few of her reviews after I'd been asked if it was OK for her to tag along with Natalie. She was a tough cookie; hence my apprehension and the turmoil that had been going on between Raffaele and me. This review was outstanding. I couldn't help but smile and sat there, almost in tears, re-reading it over and over. Once it had sunk in fully, I rushed out of the office and called to Ritchie, Jacob, Rachael and Osheena to gather round. I then read the review out to them. They all stood there, in complete silence, although the more I read, the more they smiled. As soon as I'd finished reading there was applause from all of them. Ritchie was the first to speak out, as he had also attended the opening.

"That's an unbelievably good review, brilliant and so complimentary," he said. "Have you called Raffaele yet? He must be thrilled."

"No, I can't. I went to do it, but then I remembered all the harsh words that were exchanged between us last time, and I couldn't bring myself to do it."

Ritchie and the rest of the team just nodded and looked knowingly. They'd been working with me through the pain and heartache that I'd been going through and knew only too well that I was feeling hurt, but also guilty at the way things had been left with Raffaele. Just to bring the mood of the office back into line, I offered to go and buy some cakes, by way of celebrating Raffaele's review, despite him not being there himself to appreciate our efforts to do so. Ritchie offered to go himself, but I needed some air and time to think about what to do or not to do where Raffaele was concerned.

I returned to the office with cream cakes (naughty but nice, as they say) and we all took a coffee break.

When I returned to my office there was a message sitting on my desk. It was from Timothy. The message said that he needed to talk to me urgently, though I didn't have a clue what about. Maybe his wife, Arabella, had decided yet again that heels were not for her and he needed me to give her another boost about how good she looked in them, so as to feed his shoe/foot fetish. I couldn't see how that kind of thing would be considered urgent, but then Timothy was a very odd duck when it came to high heels and his bodily reaction to them (that reminded me that I should ensure that I never wear heels around him, for fear that I might be embarrassed by his reaction). I picked up the phone and dialled his direct number.

"Hello, Timothy Robertson speaking."

"Hello Timothy, this is GiGi. I'm just returning your call."

"Oh GiGi, thank you so much for calling me back. I need to arrange a meeting with you as soon as possible, if you're available. This afternoon would be good, or even this evening? This just can't wait until tomorrow." Then he fell silent.

"Whatever's the matter, Timothy? You sound almost flustered, which is not like you at all. Is it Arabella? Has she stopped wearing the high heels? Do you want me to take her on a shopping trip to reignite her interest in them?

"No, no, it's not that at all." He pressed, "This is a business matter that I need your help on and it's a matter of some urgency." There was another pregnant pause while he waited for me to answer, not wanting to give me any further information over the phone.

"OK, I can meet you after work if that suits. It's just that with everything we have going on here currently my diary's pretty full today. I can't see myself finishing before about six-thirty pm. Would meeting at seven be OK? Somewhere where we can both eat and talk would be good, as I'll be ravenous by that time!" I suggested.

"Of course, of course; that would be perfect. Shall we say at Chez Jacqueline's at seven, then? Got to run; see you later" – and he hung up. I was intrigued by what could have made Timothy so flustered, and why it was such an urgent matter that it couldn't wait until the next day. On the one hand, I liked Timothy and Arabella, and they were good clients; on the other hand I couldn't see how I could be of any help to him with a business matter. I knew nothing about banking (other than running up credit-card debts, that is – which thankfully have now all been cleared), but I was far too busy to sit there wondering. I had clients to see and I needed to mention the matter to Ritchie, just to keep him posted that "something was afoot," as Sherlock Holmes would say.

CHAPTER 40

Ritchie had his own name for Timothy, but it isn't one I feel I can repeat. His advice was to just go along and hear him out. There was little point in trying to guess when there could be a million different reasons for Timothy wanting to meet me. I knuckled down to work and the day passed very quickly, with plenty of happy clients along the way. I even found time to go out and buy a new outfit, considering where I was going to have dinner that evening.

Six pm came and went and so had all the things I had to deal with that day. I took some time to get myself into my new outfit and spruce myself up. Then it was a mad rush to reach Chez Jacqueline's on time, although I knew Timothy wouldn't be bothered if I was fashionably late.

I arrived at the restaurant, gave my name to the maître d' and was escorted to a table by the window, at which Timothy was already seated. Being the gentleman that he was, he stood up when I reached him and waited until I was seated before he sat back down. The waiter came over and brought us an apéritif, unordered, and then we sat there chit-chatting for a while as we perused the menu. Timothy, who had obviously eaten there before, made a couple of suggestions as to what I could choose, but I decided on something else entirely. There was a dish on the menu that seemed very similar to one that Raffaele had added to his opening menu at the restaurant, and that's what I chose.

Now was I being silly still thinking about him, despite not having spoken to him for more than a week? Even after having read Caroline Porter's wonderful review of his restaurant … I couldn't decide.

I almost changed my mind, but I couldn't help wanting to taste how a competing chef cooked the dish. When the waiter returned I gave him my order, waited for him to leave, then broached the subject of why I was there and what on earth it could be that I might be able to assist a banker with in respect of his business.

Timothy wasn't at all surprised that I had jumped in with questions at the first opportunity, as soon as we were alone. He therefore got straight to the point. "Jasper and Lady Whilsham are in trouble," he said. I was gobsmacked. If you'd asked me to guess what Timothy was going to say, that's one I'd never have guessed in a million years.

"What does that have to do with me?" I asked. He then launched into what seemed like a presentation, all business-like, in an effort both to give me information and to convince me that his way of dealing with it was the right way to go. I was almost afraid he was going to start showing me PowerPoint slides. The starter came and went, with Timothy hardly having taken a bite. I was ravenous and so sat eating, listening and watching Timothy while he explained his thoughts on what to do about the Jasper situation. He stopped only occasionally, or so it seemed, to either take a breath or have a sip of his wine. He was, by that time, so animated that it wouldn't have mattered who came up to our table, be it a waiter or even Jasper himself; not even that would have stopped him. He reached a point where he'd imparted all the information and ideas that he had wanted to and so fell silent, watching me closely for my reaction.

The main course arrived then, and it was obvious to me that Timothy just wanted me to give him my opinion and answer his proposal. He decided to wait, at least until we'd eaten the main course, fortunately. There was a bit more small talk and I told him my reasons for choosing the main that I had. Timothy was now starting to get quite twitchy. My mind was spinning and I kept thinking about his proposal, at the same time trying to compare the dish I had with Raffaele's, just to go back after one second to the proposal. Too many things on my mind at the same time. Damn!

At that very moment my mobile rang. I took one look and saw that it was my mother. Bloody typical. I looked at Timothy, apologised and said, "If I don't answer this, the phone won't stop ringing for the rest of the meal." He was very understanding; despite it being obvious to me that he was on tender-hooks.

"Hello, Mum; now isn't a good time, as I'm in a very important business meeting. Would it be OK if I called you tomorrow?" I said, attempting to be business-like and even maybe a little abrupt, hoping she would understand.

"Oh, but GiGi, I really need to talk to you. Can't you even give me five minutes of your time?" (There are no such things as five-minute conversations once my Mum gets going.) "I'm sorry, Mum, but I'm having a business meal with Timothy: you remember I told you about him – the big business banker who's also a client? We're discussing something that can't wait and so I have to go now, Mum. Promise I'll talk to you tomorrow," and I hung up. I decided not to take any more chances and switched the phone off, just in case. I apologised and, just at that point, the waiter interrupted us yet again, bringing our desserts. My hunger, by that time, had been sated so I took a few moments to explain to him what my thoughts were; I felt I'd kept him waiting long enough, especially knowing that I wasn't going to be able to give him a definitive answer that evening.

"Timothy, first I'd like to thank you for bringing me to this lovely restaurant; it's certainly a far nicer place to talk business than in the boardroom back at the office. Second, and the bit you're waiting for, is that I can't give you an answer yet to your proposal. A lot has happened in the office in the past couple of weeks; as now I'm not just in partnership with Ritchie, but also with Jacob and Osheena as well. So I need to talk to all of them about this before I can give you an answer. What I will say is this: I, for one, would love to be able to see if we can make this work. It would be a fantastic opportunity for me and the team and I'm so grateful that the first person you thought of was me. For that – I thank you wholeheartedly. I do take on board the urgency of the matter – but would you be able to wait until, let's say, tomorrow late afternoon to have an answer from me?" I took a breath at this point, as it seemed to me as if I'd been talking for a month. My mind was still racing with ideas, the potential of what could be a completely new side to the business and lastly, but by no means least, being able to stick it to Jasper and Lady AboutToGoBankrupt.

Timothy, who already knew that I was in partnership with Ritchie, didn't express surprise when I mentioned that Jacob and Osheena had received shares as well. He'd come to know that I was definitely someone who not only looked after their customers, but staff as well; also, despite it cutting down my own share, I made sure that they were looked after financially. Timothy didn't even hesitate. He simply said, "I knew it was going to be a long shot, for you to make this decision without having first discussed it with Ritchie, and now I can fully understand why you need a team discussion. That was why I needed us to meet this evening, as the cut-off for being able to proceed with the proposal is the day after tomorrow. If you could give me an answer tomorrow, I can set all the wheels in motion in order to allow us to proceed late Friday afternoon. That would give us a head start on any other parties that might be interested, as the Notice isn't going to be printed in the newspapers till Monday morning. Hopefully, by that time, we should have things all sewn up."

I wondered to myself whether this was insider dealing, or something like that, but could only assume that it wasn't, as Timothy was way too straight-laced about his job to even consider doing that. It was left that, by four pm the next day at the very latest, I'd call Timothy to give him my answer. He handed me a bundle of papers and documents to peruse, and thanked me for being so understanding and for allowing him to broach his idea with me. I thanked him as well, for it had been a complete surprise to me that he regarded me highly enough to propose this venture to me in the first place.

Timothy paid the bill and we parted ways outside the restaurant, with me promising to call him the following day. My mind was agog with all the information and for once I was glad that the evening was mild, and that he'd chosen somewhere not far from where I lived to have our meeting. It was going to be a long night.

CHAPTER 41

The following morning, feeling as if I hadn't slept a wink, I arrived at the office at seven on the dot. I couldn't keep away from the place. I needed time to settle down, drink my first two or three coffees and digest all the paperwork that Timothy had given me, prior to the rest of the team arriving. It took quite some time to read again through all the details of the proposal. The team arrived, had their coffees, started working, and not one of them thought to look to see if I'd arrived yet. My office door was closed, as it usually is when I'm not in there yet, so they all thought I either had an early client appointment away from the office or had overslept.

At around about 9.45 I opened my office door. The reception I received was one of shock and surprise. Osheena was the first to speak up. "How long have you been here? Why was your office door closed? Is there something the matter?" Question after question was thrown at me, to the point where all I could do was clear my throat and hold up my hands to ask them to stop. Ritchie then stepped forward and joked, "Did you sleep in there last night? I mean, we're busy, but not that busy."

"Sort of," I answered. I took a deep breath and asked them all to join me in the boardroom, including also Rachael, who despite not having been here very long yet, needed to hear what was said, as it did also ultimately concern her as well. I could see clearly on all their faces that the suspense was almost killing them. I then suggested that they each go get their tea or coffee and I put the answerphone on, as this was going to take a while. I had a lot to explain, after all, and there was a deadline.

"Come on, spit it out!" said Ritchie, when all were assembled. "We're not in trouble again, are we?"

"No, we aren't," I said, looking at each of them with a naughty grin on my face. "Do you remember Timothy?"

"The banker with the foot fetish?" said Osheena. "You mean the ..."

"RITCHIE!" I managed to stop him before he could use those horrible words. When eventually they fell silent, I dropped the bomb.

"Timothy is part of a group of venture capitalists, who are taking over the Battersea Fashion Centre next week." I scanned their faces for a reaction. Jaws dropped; someone turned their head towards the window, in the direction of Public Enemy Number One; then a moment later, disbelief and fear.

"There's nothing to worry about. Barnes Ltd was strapped for cash; the Centre was doing OK, but not well enough to save the firm from going into debt. They overstretched themselves, so they tried to sell this building and the plot of land to a firm of builders. Unfortunately for them, the builders weren't willing to wait a couple of years until all the tenants in this building had left, so they pulled out, leaving Barnes Ltd without adequate cash flow."

Jaws dropped further.

"Timothy knows how we operate and knows many of our best clients. He wants us to run what will be the new Battersea Fashion Centre, in the exact same way as what we do here. We would also be shareholders in this new venue. We need to take a decision by today, four pm."

Silence.

More silence. And yet more silence.

And then, they started firing questions one after the other. Thank God I'd spent much of the night studying the papers.

The first was Osheena. "Would we retain our

independence?"

"As anywhere in business, if we're successful nobody will be questioning us. It's the same in this firm. In addition, we'd have shares, and structures like a marketing department, accountants – the whole shebang. And a whole fashion department store where we could pick and choose what suits our customers best."

"Would we have a say on what is exposed in the store?" This time the question came from Jacob.

"Yes. They recognise that we're successful because we care about our customers, that the core of our business is built around making our customers happy. It would be up to us to make that choice."

"Cool." Jacob was ecstatic; no more days spent scavenging for samples and clothes. We would have everything we liked to hand.

They asked a few more questions and I explained the details as best I could. It was going to be a mutual decision, and being with them, working together, was the most important thing. Although we were going mainstream, my hope was that, after all the things we'd done together, we could keep doing what we were doing as friends – like a family, I dared say.

"So, where do we sign?" Ritchie asked eventually.

I loved it. From being ejected from that place to becoming a shareholder in it … life sometimes takes unexpected turns that no one could ever possibly imagine. I looked around and could see only jubilant faces; everyone was excited about this turn of events. Now it would be up to us to make a success of it.

"Does anyone object if we merge with the Battersea Fashion Centre?" I finally asked.

"You must be kidding," said Jacob, speaking for everybody else "When are we going to get another chance like that? Go and call Timothy before he regains his senses and rethinks the whole matter."

"I can do better: I can conference him in." They deserved that; I was no longer one of the two owners of this firm, but a senior partner. They all deserved to be there. I looked up Timothy's number on my phone and dialled it from the conference phone in the room.

"Timothy Robertson speaking."

"Hello, Timothy, this is GiGi speaking."

"Hello there. Do you have any news for me?" he asked eagerly.

"I'm in the boardroom with all the other partners. We would like to accept your offer." It sounded a bit too much *Dragon's Den*, but hey, I couldn't think of a better way of accepting.

"Congratulations, then! I'll need the paperwork signed today, but don't worry – there's nothing really binding. We'll have to go through due diligence before we formalise the merger, but that gives us the opportunity to announce it. Do you have a solicitor who could work on this matter on your behalf?"

I looked around in the room and everybody had the same thought. "As a matter of fact I think we do."

"Good for him," continued Timothy. "There'll be some hefty fees coming his way. And congratulations again for your choice; you lot deserve it and it will be a great ride, that much I can assure you."

We thanked him and closed the call, everybody sighing with relief. We were going to be the biggest, fattest, happiest fashion consultant firm in the world, and we deserved it.

For an instant, I thought about all the struggles we'd had to endure, but that was the past. A new future was ahead of us, and in that very moment I knew we were going to be OK.

I passed the papers around so that everybody could read what they were signing up for, and later on that day we sent them by courier to Timothy.

Nobody really worked that afternoon; too much emotion was going around in the office. We kept going from one desk to another, starting to share ideas on what we'd be doing, what changes we would have to make to the Battersea Fashion Centre. Someone even also started wondering about their new offices.

I doubted that any of us were going to be able to sleep that night.

CHAPTER 42

You know that feeling when you want to celebrate an achievement, but you can't? I was in that state of mind. Sure – the success, the new venue, taking over the Battersea Fashion Centre, the potential of being one of the biggest fashion firms in the UK.

But still, there was something missing.

It was at that point that my mobile rang. My mother.

Oh dear, what now?

"Hello, GiGi."

"Hello Mum, how are you doing?" I asked, although I didn't really want to know.

"Oh, ups and downs as usual. D'you want to come around later on? I've prepared a shepherd's pie and I made far too much. You know, at our age we can't afford to eat all that; we're getting old. You'd be welcome."

Hang on. No nagging? Just a dinner invite? Hmmm. There must be a trick here, I thought.

"OK, you know it's my favourite. See you later, then?"

"I'll count on it. Don't work too hard. Ta-ta."

"Bye, Mum."

Something was going on and I couldn't put my finger on it. Was I going to walk into a trap? But frankly I hadn't seen them in a while, and it being Saturday I had no excuses. I couldn't even think of one, and to be honest I hadn't wanted to, as I felt guilty for not having rung her following her call when I was in my meeting with Timothy. She was my mother, after all. So I changed into a dress and drove to their place. There were moments where my mother was a really pleasant person, with even a witty sense of humour; it was just that during this last period she'd seemed to get on my nerves more than usual.

I arrived at their house at around half past four and immediately started thinking about an exit strategy. Maybe some sort of fashion emergency, or a wedding going wrong. Never go into *Dragon's Den* without knowing the facts, your numbers and, most of all, without an exit strategy.

"Hello, Mum," I said once she'd opened the door. We kissed on the cheek and she let me in. Ronald, my stepfather, was busy reading the papers, but as soon as he heard my voice he came to greet me.

"Come in, come in; it's been ages since you were here for dinner. The shepherd's pie has just gone in the oven, so we have a little time to catch up." My parents, owing to their ages and suffering from indigestion if they ate too late, liked to eat at around six pm, so my timing might have been a little off if I planned a hasty exit!

I could smell the pie from where I stood; it was a divine sensation. I've never been a great cook (I'm rubbish at it actually, as you already know), but I had no problem whatsoever in recognising good food when I could smell it or taste it.

"Let's go to the kitchen and have a glass of wine," suggested Ronald. Wise man. "So how's business? We've heard rumours."

I knew that. They'd decided to trap me here, stick a pie under my nose, knowing full well I couldn't resist, and then, BAM! Start with the interrogation, how it would have been risky and so on. My mother should have worked for the CIA or for MI6 in the service of Her Majesty. She didn't have a grapevine; she had a whole bloody vineyard.

"Indeed. We're going to merge with the Battersea Fashion Centre next month. It's really going to happen," I said, with pride in my voice.

"What about that boyfriend of yours, Raffaele?" my mother asked suddenly. "You stopped talking about him very abruptly."

"That's because we split up," I retorted, "Apparently I was working too hard and we didn't spend enough time together. He just didn't want to have a workaholic around."

"So the main issue was that you were working too hard and didn't see each other often enough?" asked Ronald.

Put like that, I sounded like a career bitch: someone who wouldn't care about a partner in order to achieve her goals, now that we were elaborating about that.

"You could always slow down a bit," my mother said. "You have some very capable people, like your friend Ritchie, working with you. Believe me, being successful is important, but what's the point, if you don't have someone to share your life with?"

"And you're still in love; I can see that from the way you talk about him," added Ronald. Love had never been an issue; I was madly in love with Raffaele, but somehow I'd never been able to balance my working life with my private one. I had a burning desire to be successful, which could have roots going back to my mother not considering that I could make it on my own, but the price to pay was perhaps too high.

"You might not mind it now, because you're young and full of energy, but maybe later on you'll look back and regret not giving that nice guy a chance," said.my mother. "Or in a few years you might meet him with his new family and think,

'What if it was me; the one living with him?' But by then it would be too late."

It was hurtful; plain and simple, but hurtful. I was dedicating all my energy to my company, but when the job was done, with whom could I share the results, if I was alone? I hated to admit it, but Mother was right. She's not always right: when it's a matter of choosing colours that gel, sometimes she's rubbish and old-fashioned, but on this subject she was right. Damn! Working wasn't enough; I had to balance my time better. Working was a means to achieve something else, such as love, a family, spending time with that very person that makes you feel special.

"I suppose so. I'll think about that," I answered.

"Of course you will, my dear. Now let's sit, because the pie is just about ready."

We finished our dinner and I enjoyed the carefree moments we were sharing; it was a shame Rachel wasn't there. Moments like that, when you're with the people you love, are worthwhile; they make you realise why we all work so hard and what the true values in our lives are. Being with the people you love is the most important thing; the rest can come later.

I was shaking when I finally drove away. For a while I kept wandering without a clear direction; I drove down street after street in the direction of the office, but I was sure I didn't want to go there. That was also the source of my problem. Suddenly I realised what I had to do. I changed direction and went to see my best friend.

When Ritchie opened the door he was surprised to see me there, unannounced. "GiGi, what are you doing here?"

"We need to talk. May I come in?"

And so we talked, and then we talked some more. He asked a number of times if I was sure. I was.

CHAPTER 43

I didn't mind driving, especially that evening. I reached the Gastro Pub when it was almost eleven in the evening. I wasn't hungry; I had just one thought on my mind. When I entered the premises Simon, one of the waiters, came to greet me and asked if he could help. I said not; I would just have a glass of wine at the bar, maybe some nibbles, and wait until Raffaele finished in the kitchen.

The restaurant was buzzing despite the late hour. I had no doubt Raffaele would have made it work; he was a talented chef and he deserved it. I also recognised a few faces from the opening, meaning that he'd started having repeat customers. Good.

Suddenly a familiar voice reached me from behind. "GiGi, what are you doing here?"

I turned and faced Raffaele. Oh my gosh: he was so beautiful (I fully appreciate that when describing a man the correct term was handsome, but …). "We need to talk, I'll just wait here till you've finished."

"No need for that. Give me one minute and I'll let the rest of the kitchen staff take over."

I felt guilty about interrupting him during his work, but at the same time I was grateful I wouldn't have to wait another couple of hours. He came back and signalled to me to follow him into his office, at the back of the restaurant.

"What's going on?" he asked.

"Raffaele, I do love you," I started.

"I love you too – but that was never the point, was it?"

"We're going to be merging with the Battersea Fashion Centre."

A look of disbelief showed on his face. "You're going to work with Jasper?"

"No, nothing like that!" And then I described to him all that had happened, from the bloggers, the court hearing, the attempt to bribe us, until Timothy's offer.

"The same Timothy who came here for the opening?" he asked.

"The one and only."

"He's actually become an established customer. And he brings lots of people, too," he said, as if for a moment he was pondering a long list of clients.

"So, you'll be extremely busy."

"No, I won't. It's time for me to take a step back. I spoke to Ritchie today and he'll be the one to take the lead on the new venture. He's capable and he deserves it. I'll still work there, of course, but I won't be the one making the hard decisions and working until late any more. I actually think I might go part time and enjoy the earnings from my shares."

He looked at me in disbelief. "Are you saying …?"

"Yes, I am. I love that job, but there are more important things in life, I want to be with you, the person that I love; to grow old and spend quality time together. That is, if you haven't changed your mind about wanting to be with me."

He jumped out of his chair and hugged me in those strong arms of his. "Of course I haven't changed my mind." We looked each other in the eye and then kissed passionately.

"I'll have time to spend with you and cook you a nice dinner," I laughed.

"No way. I've already tried one of your experiments and surely I do not want to make that mistake again. Maybe I could teach you," he added.

That wasn't such a bad idea. "Maybe you can cook and I can take photos and put your dishes into a book. We could send the first copy to Caroline Porter." "We both laughed, and all the tension that had accumulated between us during the past few weeks disappeared. We were back where we had left off, happy and in love.

"I want at least two kids. I don't mind if they're girls or boys, as long as they have your eyes," he added.

"Deal!"

You know, even the Dragons keep saying how important their families are.

* * * * *

BLUE AND GREEN SHOULD NEVER BE SEEN!

I just wanted to say thank you for purchasing this my debut novel.

Before you go off and hunt for your next great read I would very much appreciate you leaving feedback on the website you purchased it from.

If you want to keep up with the news of what is coming next please check my website at www.colettekebell.com to find out more.

You can also find my author pages at

https://www.goodreads.com/ColetteKebell

or

https://www.facebook.com/pages/Colette-Kebell/882613368417057

Or join me on twitter @colettekebell

I am still writing as I have enjoyed writing this as much as I hope you have enjoyed reading it. Thank you once again for buying my book and hopefully those that are to follow.